"I am staying in the palace tonight in the same wing as you," Nathaniel said quietly, his breath blowing against the sensitive lobe of her ear.

"How..." It was a fight to breathe, let alone talk. "How do you know which wing I'm in?"

"Because I made it my business to know." He inhaled deeply and she knew it was her scent he took in so greedily.

He kept his hold on her hand as he stepped back and gazed down at her.

He had a magnetism she had felt from their first introduction all those years ago.

He was the only man she had ever wondered about...

"At one o'clock I will come to your door." He pressed a kiss to her knuckles. "I know your companion has the adjoining room, so I will not knock. I will be there but I will leave our fate in your hands. If you don't open it, I will go back to my room and you can pretend I was never there. But before you make the decision of whether or not to open the door, ask yourself this—when was the last time you did something solely for yourself that wasn't bound up in duty? You're a princess, Catalina, but tonight I can teach you how to be a woman, too."

One Night With Consequences

When one night...leads to pregnancy!

When succumbing to a night of unbridled desire, it's impossible to think past the morning after!

But, with the sheets barely settled, that little blue line appears on the pregnancy test and it doesn't take long to realize that one night of white-hot passion has turned into a lifetime of consequences!

Only one question remains:

How do you tell a man you've just met that you're about to share more than just his bed?

Find out in:

Look for more ***One Night With Consequences***
coming soon!

Michelle Smart

———

CLAIMING HIS CHRISTMAS
CONSEQUENCE

HHARLEQUIN PRESENTS®

Recycling programs
for this product may
not exist in your area.

ISBN-13: 978-0-373-13481-6

Claiming His Christmas Consequence

First North American Publication 2016

Copyright © 2016 by Michelle Smart

Printed in U.S.A.

Michelle Smart's love affair with books started when she was a baby, when she would cuddle them in her cot. A voracious reader of all genres, she found her love of romance established when she stumbled across her first Harlequin book at the age of twelve. She's been reading (and writing) them ever since. Michelle lives in Northamptonshire with her husband and two young smarties.

Books by Michelle Smart

Harlequin Presents

The Russian's Ultimatum
The Rings That Bind
The Perfect Cazorla Wife

Wedlocked!

Wedded, Bedded, Betrayed

The Kalliakis Crown

Talos Claims His Virgin
Theseus Discovers His Heir
Helios Crowns His Mistress

Society Weddings

The Greek's Pregnant Bride

The Irresistible Sicilians

What a Sicilian Husband Wants
The Sicilian's Unexpected Duty
Taming the Notorious Sicilian

Visit the Author Profile page at Harlequin.com for more titles.

To Geoff & Jan with thanks and love for all
the support and encouragement xxx

CHAPTER ONE

'YOU WERE RIGHT to end your engagement,' Nathaniel Giroud murmured, nodding lazily at the dance floor where Prince Helios and his bride were dancing together, clearly enjoying themselves. 'Helios would have made you unhappy.'

Princess Catalina Fernandez took a long drink of her champagne. There was the faintest tremor in her hand. 'How can you be so sure?'

'No chemistry.' He paused before adding, 'Not like the chemistry between you and I.'

Her heart-shaped chin pointed forward and she pushed her chair back from the table they were sitting alone at, the motion sending a small waft of her sultry scent into his path.

He longed to smell every part of her.

'We cannot have this conversation,' she said quietly. 'What you are implying is impossible.'

He rested a hand on hers before she could get to her feet. 'Why is it impossible?'

'You know why.' She slid her hand away and met his

gaze. 'I must save myself for my husband. My purity is my gift for him.'

'A gift?' The concept was so ludicrous he almost laughed but this was no laughing matter. He thought of Catalina's brother, heir to the throne of Monte Cleure, sleeping his way around Europe without an ounce of penitence, allowing himself—and being allowed by their father—all the hedonistic delights he would deny his own sister on account of nothing more than the fact she had been born a woman.

Now she'd been dumped by Helios, whatever the sanitised whitewash of the official press release might have said, the rumours suggested she was promised to an aging Swedish duke. Nathaniel had no qualms about seducing her. Catalina wanted him. He knew it. And she knew it too.

'So you are nothing but a possession?'

Confusion flittered in her dark eyes.

'Is that what you're saying?' he pressed. 'That you don't have autonomy over your own body? Are you nothing but a vessel for the next generation?'

'It isn't like that. I am a princess. This is my life. It's what I was born to be.'

'You are also a woman.'

Her delicate throat moved.

He leaned a little closer, brushing his arm against hers, moving in for the kill.

Princess Catalina was a breed apart from all women. That she had class and poise went without saying but she was also incredibly beautiful too. And she carried herself with such stillness. Looking at her was like gazing at a portrait come to life. Tall and raven-haired with sultry eyes like melted chocolate, she had skin that seemed never to have sat in the sun, like clear, flawless alabaster. Today she was dressed beautifully in a knee-length peach dress that emphasised her full breasts and tiny waist without showing an inch of unnecessary flesh. Her hair had been piled into a wide, round bun on the top of her head, the effect of it all bringing to mind sixties glamour. It was a look only she could pull off.

She was a woman without flaws.

But, of course, every person in the world had flaws, and he itched to discover what hers could be.

The rumours that her father, the King of Monte Cleure, was planning to snub Helios's wedding had proven true. With Catalina's brother now having disappeared with his latest pneumatically enhanced girlfriend, Nathaniel knew this would be his one and only shot with her.

'Your first time should be special. It should be with a man who will worship you and take care of you, not some cold-blooded aristocrat doing his duty.'

'I'm an aristocrat,' she said, the same quiver he could feel in her delectable body so close to his own echoing in her voice.

'Ah, but you're different—beneath your icy exterior runs blood of lava.'

Spotting the Swedish duke making his way to their table, Nathaniel stood up.

Catalina stared at him, obviously confused by his abruptness.

'Your rumoured fiancé is heading our way. I suspect he's going to ask you to dance.'

Her gaze flitted to the aging duke.

'He's not my fiancé.' She gave a long exhale. 'Not yet.'

'Then there is nothing to stop you dancing with me.' He extended his hand to her, palm up.

Now her throat moved in an obvious swallow. 'My brother told me to stay away from you.'

He'd just bet he had. 'Do you always do what your brother tells you?'

'Yes.'

He raised a brow and murmured, 'And do you always *want* to do as you're told?'

There was the slightest shake of her head.

The duke was only paces away from their table.

Suddenly, her hand shot out to take Nathaniel's and in one graceful movement, she rose to her feet.

Her eyes darted to the dance floor as if she were searching for someone, before she looked at him and said, 'One dance.'

He bowed his head. 'If you insist.'

Her lips twitched. 'It has to be just one dance. I have to think of my reputation. There are spies everywhere.'

One dance was good enough for him. Not giving her time to change her mind, Nathaniel led her to the dance floor, leaving the duke staring at their retreating backs with a scratch of his balding head.

When he found a spot for them, he kept her hand entwined in his, pulled her close and snaked his free arm around her waist, resting his hand above the lining of her dress so it lay against her bare back. Her skin had the texture of creamy silk.

She fitted into his arms perfectly.

The added height from her heels meant her head rested perfectly in the crook of his neck. He could smell the expensive scent of her shampoo, mingling so deliciously with the sultry perfume that drove his senses wild.

He pressed himself a little closer, close enough that she would be able to feel his racing heart.

'Relax,' he murmured, stroking her rigid back. 'I don't bite.'

But I think I want you to...

During Catalina's short courtship to Helios and their even shorter engagement, they had danced together many times. She had never felt *anything* like this. Her heart had never beaten so fast that she could feel it clamouring against her ribs.

The heat that had steadily built in her most intimate area that day under Nathaniel's relentless attention spread through her pores, a tingling desire that thrilled and terrified her in equal measure.

She'd seen desire for herself when she'd been an impressionable fifteen-year-old. The beauty of the moment had eventually counteracted the horror of *who* she had found in desire's throes, awakening something inside her; a yearning...a wish...

Oh, how she had hoped she would feel it with Helios but the chemistry between them had been non-existent. The chemistry between herself and the duke was even less.

The skin on her back whirred under Nathaniel's touch. She could feel every bump of his hand, the pads of his fingers. That yearning…that wish…heavens, she was *feeling* it.

But all too soon their one dance was over.

Catalina took a deep breath and made to step away but his hold tightened.

'I am staying in the palace tonight in the same wing as you,' he said quietly, the words whispering against the sensitive lobe of her ear.

'How…?' It was a fight to breathe, let alone talk. 'How do you know which wing I'm in?'

'Because I made it my business to know.' He inhaled deeply and she knew it was her scent he breathed in so greedily.

He kept his hold on her hand as he stepped back and gazed down at her.

At thirty-five Nathaniel's face was a craggy cast of crinkles and lines, his impossibly tall body hard and rangy, testament to a man who enjoyed a varied outdoor life. His nose was strong and bumpy, his eyes that always seemed to spark with amusement were a pale green and he had a generous mouth that smiled often to create a dimple in his left cheek. Topping it all off was short brown hair that seemed to fight any attempt to be neat.

He had a magnetism which she had felt from their first introduction all those years ago.

He was the only man she had ever wondered about…

'At one o'clock I will come to your door.' He pressed a kiss to her knuckles. 'I know your companion has the adjoining room so I will not knock. I will be there but I will leave our fate in your hands. If you don't open the door I will go back to my room and you can pretend I was never there. But before you make the decision of whether or not to open it, ask yourself this—when was the last time you did something solely for yourself that wasn't bound up in duty? You're a princess, Catalina, but tonight I can teach you how to be a woman too.'

And with those words, he let go of her hand, bowed, and left the dance floor.

Three weeks later.

The stick with the pink line stared at Princess Catalina Fernandez mockingly.

Merry Christmas, Catalina. Here's your surprise present.

All the poise she had spent twenty-five years perfecting had gone. All she felt now was a rabid terror eating her from the inside out.

Two blissful minutes when Nathaniel had entered her for the first time without protection before he'd withdrawn and sheathed himself. Two minutes of madness.

What was she going to do?

The nausea swelled up again and she retched, but her stomach was now so empty all that came out was bile. She didn't know if it was the terror causing it or the new hormones taking over her body.

She brushed her teeth for the third time that morning but could still taste the acid on her tongue. She patted her face dry and stared at her reflection, trying desperately to force a smile to her pale face. In six hours she would sit down with her family for their Christmas feast. Aunts, uncles, cousins; those who worked at the palace and those that didn't. They would all be there.

She breathed deeply, the exhalation coming out in ragged movements from lungs that seemed to have closed in shock.

A knock on her bedroom door brought her to her senses.

That would be Marion, her cousin and chief companion. Marion had brought Catalina's breakfast to her earlier—the tray still remained untouched—and now would be ready to draw her bath.

She couldn't confide in her. Marion had a sly side that Catalina had never warmed to. When she'd come of age and had been permitted to appoint her own 'companions', a House of Fernandez euphemism for personal staff, she'd been obligated to take Marion on. In a palace full of servants, personal staff always came from family, and Marion's mother was sister to Catalina's father.

She counted to five in her head and composed herself. Not with a single whisper of body language would she show that anything was amiss.

Stepping back into her room, she called out 'Come in,' and sat down at her dresser.

Except it wasn't Marion who opened the door. It was her brother, Dominic.

There was nothing festive about the look on his face.

'So...' he said silkily, closing the door behind him. 'It's true. You're pregnant.'

Thank goodness she was already seated or her shaky legs would have given way.

When the test had shown itself positive only half an hour ago she had known she wouldn't be able to keep this a secret for long but she'd hoped for a few days' grace.

She clamped her lips together and nodded. There was no point in lying. And little point in wondering how he knew. Privacy was an alien concept when it came to the female members of the House of Fernandez. Not trusting Marion, Catalina had been forced to take Aliana, a second cousin and one of her newer companions, into her confidence and had sent her out to get a pregnancy test. Aliana, barely eighteen, had left the palace on the pretext of some last minute Christmas shopping, promising to keep it a secret.

But nothing in the palace remained a secret for long. To keep one required a mental strength most people didn't have, not when the King and his heir had a palace full of spies and the power to use the knowledge they gained to their advantage.

Catalina had kept her one true and most precious secret by never telling a soul.

Dominic took in her appearance with a critical sneer, then, without any warning, whipped his hand through the air and slapped her cheek. Hard. 'Merry Christmas.'

Catalina didn't allow herself to react, nor did she place a hand to her stinging flesh. Any response would give him what he wanted.

He loved nothing more than making her cry. He fed off it.

She hadn't cried in front of him since their mother's funeral seven years ago.

Suddenly she wished, with a desperation she hadn't felt since the funeral that her mother were there. Just so she would be able to hold her and receive her words of comfort. How she missed her soft voice and gentle smile.

She even wished Isabella were there but her younger sister had escaped the House of Fernandez's Christmas festivities to spend the period with her husband's family.

'Who's the father?'

She pressed her lips together.

'A virgin conception? How fitting.' His mouth curved into another hateful sneer. 'Nathaniel Giroud?'

Despite her best efforts, she couldn't stop the little tremor that raced through her at the mention of Nathaniel's name.

'It *is* him.'

Such was the fury that spread across her brother's face Catalina braced herself for another strike.

Instead, Dominic stooped down, close enough for her to smell his rancid breath. 'You disgusting *slut.*'

She didn't react. She *wouldn't* react. It would only make matters worse. She didn't even flinch when his spittle flew into her face.

'Bad enough Helios dumped you, a pure-blood royal princess, for a commoner and that the whole world knows it, whatever the press release we issued might have said, but for you to then open your legs for that piece of scum…?' Malice shone on his face. 'You realise Johann was preparing to ask Father for your hand in marriage? That's another prospect ruined.'

Bile crept up her throat, threatening to choke her.

'*You're* ruined; you know that? Johann won't want you now you're second-hand goods.'

She couldn't breathe.

'Giroud won't want you either,' Dominic jeered. 'He screwed you to get one up on me. You were nothing but a game to him and an easy lay. I told you to stay away from him and now you must pay the price.'

He stared down at her, his face twisted in an ugly contortion. 'Father will wish to speak to you. He will decide what needs to be done and what the consequences are to be.'

He made to leave then paused, turning back around to slap her other cheek. 'That's for disobeying me when I told you to stay away from Nathaniel Giroud.'

Straightening his tie, he left the room.

Alone, Catalina closed her eyes and took a long, deep breath.

The screams in her head rang out.

Placing a protective hand to her stomach, she forced herself to look in her dressing-table mirror. Bright red finger marks marred both her cheeks.

There was no way to fix the damage before Marion came to her rooms. All the same, she applied foundation with shaking hands, hoping to tone down the worst of it.

Breathe, Catalina, breathe.

When Nathaniel had left her room that morning three weeks ago, she had felt an inexplicable wrench to see the door close behind him.

She hadn't heard from him since and she hadn't expected to. They had both known it could only ever be for one night.

But she'd been aware of him for years.

Friends with the Kalliakis Princes, if not Catalina's own brother, Nathaniel had often attended the same functions she'd been at; a tall magnetic figure her eyes had always been drawn to. She'd experienced a little pull in the pit of her stomach whenever she'd met his eye and experienced an even greater tug whenever they'd greeted each other with the kiss on both cheeks that everyone used. But she had never allowed herself to think anything about it. They were part of the same social network but they were not friends. Male friends were not permitted for a princess from the House of Fernandez.

Until Helios's wedding, when Nathaniel had taken it upon himself to act as her guardian angel on the day that should have been *her* wedding, she had never exchanged more than pleasantries with him.

He was intensely private, so she knew little about him other than that his parents had died in an accident when he was very young—she didn't know the details—and that he'd been raised by an uncle and had attended the same boarding school as Dominic and the Kalliakis Princes. He owned a string of hotels and business developments, along with the Club Giroud, a private members club for the most affluent, which had made him one of France's richest men and a self-made billionaire before he'd turned thirty. Gregarious and charming, he was a notorious womaniser and hell-raiser, someone who enjoyed the lifestyle his wealth brought to its fullest extent.

But he'd shown a different side to her that day. He'd seen that she was vulnerable and had made it his mission to get her through the wedding with a smile on her face. Whether his motive from the outset had been to bed her, she didn't care. She'd wanted him too. For the one and only time in her life she'd thrown caution to the wind and embraced a side she'd spent a lifetime suppressing.

Even if she hadn't been a princess and he a commoner whom her brother detested, she would never have expected more than one night. Commitment was an alien concept to him.

But she hadn't been able to get him from her mind. Every time she closed her eyes she could see him. She could taste him. She could feel his skin under her fingers. In the privacy of her bed she would relive their night together, playing it over like a movie in her head. Every touch. Every caress.

She had assumed the next time she would see him would be at some function or other. She had assumed he would greet her with the usual kiss and that maybe his hand would press into her side a little longer than normal, a subtle acknowledgement of their time together. She had assumed she would hug their secret to herself for the rest of her life.

Since she could remember, it had been made plain her virginity was sacred, something to be saved for her wedding day. For twenty-five years she had accepted this.

She was a princess. She had a life of wealth and privilege. She was a representative of the House of Fernandez, expected to marry into a family that would strengthen her own family's cultural links and power. She was expected to behave with decorum and propriety at all times and not once had she failed in this. She had never whispered a word of complaint that her brother was allowed to do whatever he wanted with whomever he wanted and neither had she complained that free spirit Isabella's bratty behaviour was indulged by their brother and father alike.

Dominic had never raised a finger to Isabella.

Not once in her life had Catalina ever done anything that wasn't for the good of the House of Fernandez. Not once.

And then she had.

She had cast aside duty for one forbidden night.

And now she would be punished for that moment of blissful madness for the rest of her life.

What she didn't know and couldn't begin to predict was what that punishment would entail.

Christmas was the one time of year Nathaniel detested. All that fake bonhomie, the commercialisation, the forced proximity with so-called loved ones. All of it.

It brought home as nothing else did that the three people Nathaniel had loved with all his heart were gone, had been dead now for twenty-eight years. On Christmas morning, the time traditionally spent opening presents and leaving a trail of discarded wrapping paper everywhere, the loss felt as fresh as it had the first morning he'd woken without them.

This year he'd made the decision to spend the period in Monte Cleure rather than in any of his other homes. Other than the fact it was the site of his most current development, Monte Cleure had a relatively temperate winter climate, situated as it was on France's southern border with Spain, meaning there was little to no chance of snow.

He'd avoided snow for twenty-eight years.

The only sign of festivity in his apartment was the empty bottle of Scotch on the floor by the sofa, which was where he found himself when he was rudely awakened early on Boxing Day morning by the shrill tone of the intercom.

He sat bolt upright, clutching his pounding head and cursing himself for not making it to his bed. If he hadn't given his household staff four days off each to spend the holidays with their families, he would let one of them deal with the caller.

Stumbling to his feet, he punched the intercom.

'Yes?' he growled. He'd left instructions with the concierge that he was not to be disturbed until tomorrow when the madness of Christmas was over.

'Monsieur Giroud, His Highness Prince Dominic from the House of Fernandez is here to see you.'

'What does he want?'

The concierge's voice dropped to a scared murmur. 'It is not my place to ask.' Nathaniel might be the boss and owner of the entire building, but Dominic was heir to the throne of the entire country.

Nathaniel left unsaid his thought that the Prince might not be such a self-satisfied moron if people asked questions of him.

'Send him up.'

While he waited for the elevator to bring Dominic to him, he staggered to the kitchen and downed a pint of water.

Whatever the Prince wanted could not be good.

A loud rap on the door announced his arrival.

Nathaniel pulled the door open. The burly figure of the heir to the Monte Cleure throne strode in, followed closely by a bodyguard.

'What can I do for you, Dominic?' he asked, deliberately not using his title. Then, also deliberately, he turned his back and walked through to the living area. 'Here to celebrate some festive cheer with me?'

When there was no answer, he said, 'Can I offer you a drink?'

'From the look and smell of you, you've already had enough to drink,' Dominic sneered. He had the air of a junior silverback making a show of asserting its dominance. If his head didn't hurt so much, Nathaniel would find it amusing.

'If I'd known you were coming I would have showered. So, drink?'

'I'm not here for a social visit.'

'I didn't imagine you were. However, I am of the opinion that even the most boring business conversation can be sweetened with a pot of fresh Columbian coffee.' It could only help his pounding head.

'I'm not here for a business meeting either.'

'Then why don't you tell me what's so urgent you turn up unannounced at my home demanding an audience.'

'*Your* home?'

'Bought and paid for. The title deeds to the Ravensberg building are held with my lawyer if you wish to see them?' Nathaniel hadn't rented since the first apartment he'd had when he'd been seventeen and his landlord had dragged his heels over fixing the broken heating system during a particularly cold spell.

He liked to be master of his own destiny, reliant only on himself. All his properties, business and personal alike—and he had so many he'd lost count—were solely his. He didn't owe a cent to any person, bank or organisation. His business was his and his alone. No one could take it away from him. Bricks and mortar he could count on; permanent fixtures in a fragile world full of horrors.

'Title deeds are only worth something if you own the land the property is built upon. Take your development here in my country for example.'

'For sure,' he agreed amiably. He knew it infuriated Dominic that his father had overridden his objections and granted Nathaniel all the necessary permissions. 'But I think you will need to use a different example with which to make your point. I always purchase the land itself for any development I undertake.'

Nathaniel was over halfway through the construction of a hotel and business complex that would be Monte Cleure's highest landmark. It was his most ambitious project to date, a skyscraper of magnificence and beauty. *Architect Monthly* magazine had declared it a potential contender for Building of the Decade.

So far he had invested one hundred million euros in the development and fully expected to spend the same amount again by the time the project was complete.

'Now why don't we stop all this pussy-footing around and you tell me why you're here, and then I can go back to bed?'

'My sister.'

'Which one?' he asked with a nonchalant shrug, although his head immediately began to whirl.

Dominic swelled up like an overinflated balloon, and his eyes grew cruel and dark. 'Catalina.'

Nathaniel made sure to keep his features neutral.

He hadn't breathed a word about his night with the Princess. Not to anyone. He didn't for a moment think Catalina would have spoken of it either, not when she had her virginal reputation to protect. From the moment she'd admitted him into her room she'd made it clear it was something that could never be spoken of or alluded to.

It had been the perfect one-night stand, one in which there would never be any danger of the woman waking in the morning and dropping casual hints about getting together another time.

He'd left Catalina's room as the sun had risen, both of them knowing their goodbye kiss would be their last.

What they'd shared had been one incredible night that could never be repeated.

Dominic had to be here on a fishing expedition. His

spies had probably reported that Nathaniel and Catalina had danced together at Helios's wedding.

He hadn't seen her since. She hadn't attended Helios and Amy's Coronation last week. A few discreet enquires had determined that she'd had a stomach bug...

Something cold snaked up his spine.

He leaned back in his chair and inhaled. 'What about her?'

Dominic's eyes glittered with malice. 'She's pregnant.'

CHAPTER TWO

NATHANIEL'S HEART SHUDDERED to a halt.

His brain whirled and it took a few beats before he found his voice. 'Catalina's pregnant?'

Immediately his mind flew to those first glorious moments when he'd abandoned an adulthood of protection to enter her unsheathed.

What had he been *thinking*?

This could be a joke. A trap. It was no secret that Dominic hated him. Their mutual loathing had been a fixture of their lives since their schooldays.

'Yes, you sick playboy. My "virgin" sister is pregnant and you're the father.'

The way Dominic emphasised the word virgin made Nathaniel's fingers itch to punch him. He restrained himself, sinking onto a sofa, hooking one ankle over his knee and folding his arms loosely across his chest in a pose he knew would infuriate the Prince far more than physical threats of violence.

'What makes you think I'm the father?'

'She's admitted it. She sent one of her companions to get a pregnancy test for her. A different companion—

one with more loyalty to the House of Fernandez—was suspicious and found the box hidden in her rooms. She informed me immediately.'

Every curse Nathaniel had ever learnt in every language he'd ever been taught flew through his mind.

'Catalina took the test yesterday morning. Our personal physician did an additional test that also came back positive. Merry Christmas. My sister is pregnant and you're the father.'

'Where is she?' He would not take Dominic's word for anything, let alone something of such importance. 'I want to see her.'

'She's at the palace. As you can imagine, the news quite ruined Christmas for us.'

'My heart bleeds for you.'

Dominic gave a cruel smile. 'Father and I have discussed the matter in great detail. Catalina can still have a future within the House of Fernandez but first we need to contain this situation. You will be required to marry her for a limited time to legitimise the child.'

Nathaniel laughed.

Was it possible he was locked in some alcohol-induced nightmare?

'Oh, I'm being very serious.' Dominic finally took a seat, spreading his legs out in a way meant to convey dominance. 'You will marry her or you will find the title deeds to your development revoked and the building repossessed by the palace. The Ravensberg building will also be repossessed.'

'Are you threatening me?'

Dominic paused before answering, clearly unnerved

by Nathaniel's placid tone. 'I'm simply telling you of the consequences. I can have you removed from Monte Cleure at the snap of my fingers.'

'I'm sure you can.'

A malevolent expression spread over the Prince's face.

'The stupidity of some people really does astound me.' Nathaniel shook his head sadly. 'To think someone would threaten to take away land legally bought and bring a halt to a development that will boost Monte Cleure's economy exponentially... Why would someone make threats like that? If word was to get out that land legitimately purchased could be snatched away at the whim of a despot ruler, who would want to invest in such a place? Why would someone put their whole economy in peril?'

Dominic turned puce. 'Nothing would give me greater pleasure than to confiscate your land and expel you from our country and to hell with the consequences. We would recover from any short-term financial hit. However, my father will not allow a bastard to be born into the House of Fernandez. Catalina has brought enough shame to our family in recent months...'

'What, by ending her engagement to Helios?' Nathaniel said scornfully, cutting him off. 'Was she supposed to marry him knowing he loved someone else?'

'We both know Helios ended it, whatever the world was told. If Catalina had done her duty and held his interest she would never have been dumped for a common whore and would now be Queen of Agon.'

How Nathaniel stopped himself from punching Dominic square in the face he would never know.

'Your sister has spent her whole life doing her duty.'

'Clearly not or we wouldn't be having this conversation.' Dominic straightened in his chair. 'And it's not just Helios—Father had found another suitor for her.'

'The Swedish duke?' He felt fleeting satisfaction at the way Dominic's lips tightened with displeasure as he realised Nathaniel was privy to private palace information.

'Yes. Another excellent prospect ruined. If the matter were left to me, Catalina would be cut off, but my father takes a slightly different view. He's of the opinion she still adds value to our royal family and is prepared to give her one last chance to redeem herself. And that's where you come in. Either you marry her or she *will* be cut off. She will be thrown out of the palace without a single cent to support her.'

Nathaniel shrugged. 'Do it. I'll support her and the baby.'

Now Dominic's malevolence shone so brightly it almost glowed. 'How? Catalina will be forbidden from leaving the country. Her passport will be revoked. She will be forbidden from opening a bank account. She will be homeless and penniless, and you will be deported and banned from re-entering Monte Cleure—orders will be issued for your immediate arrest if you set foot on our soil.'

'You would do that to your *sister*?' Nathaniel thought back to his own sister, who had died with their parents all those years ago. If she'd lived she would now be thirty-three. He didn't remember her clearly but remembered the intensity of the sibling relationship. It sickened him that Dominic could be so evil towards his own flesh and blood.

A huge pang of guilt rent through him.

This was all his fault. He should have left Catalina alone. He'd taken advantage of her vulnerability at the wedding where she should have been the bride and not a mere guest. He could have left her alone but the opportunity to bed the one woman he'd thought would be unobtainable for ever had been impossible to resist. Even knowing of her virginity hadn't deterred him in his pursuit.

But he hadn't expected *this* consequence.

And Catalina...

She must be terrified.

No one can know. Those had been her whispered words as she'd let him into her room, before placing her fingers to her lips and pointing to the adjoining door that led to the room her chaperone—sorry, companion—had been sleeping in.

It had been like a game. A game with unimaginable consequences.

'You forget who rules this land. This isn't a democracy; my father's word is law. There is nowhere to turn for appeal.'

'You're enjoying this, aren't you?' Nathaniel held onto his veneer of calm by a whisker. 'Is this revenge for Jenna?'

A twitch passed over Dominic's face. 'This has nothing to do with Jenna.'

'I would hope not. It was nearly twenty years ago.'

'And in another twenty years I will still hate you for it. Jenna was *mine*.'

'What can I say?' Nathaniel shrugged. 'She threw herself at me.'

The all-girls' sixth form college that shared their boarding school's facilities had been invited to the Christmas party. Hormones had run rife.

They'd been caught semi-naked when Dominic had burst into the room. The house master had quickly arrived and broken up the fight before any real damage could be done. Both boys had been hauled before the headmaster. Dominic had been sent to bed. Nathaniel, whose family had neither titles nor power or even much money, had been expelled on the spot.

He'd been sent back to France and back into the care of his uncle and his uncle's wife.

That night of hijinks and hormones had lit the fuse to a chain of events that continued to affect his life to this day.

It sickened him that that one incident had the potential to ruin Catalina's life too.

'You've always been an obnoxious, arrogant ba—' Dominic seemed to remember they had an audience, glancing at his bodyguard who stood propped against the wall in the corner of the room.

His face as red as a tomato, Dominic continued, 'This is not about Jenna or my sister. This is about the House of Fernandez.'

'Catalina's a loyal member of it.'

'Not with a bastard in her belly she isn't. Unless you marry her and legitimise the pregnancy, she will be *nothing*. She will be worth nothing.'

Nathaniel thought hard and quickly. Dominic's demand that he marry Catalina came from his father, the King.

The threat to his business interests in Monte Cleure was bad enough but Catalina…

Her safety and the safety of the tiny cluster of cells in her womb were not things he could play a game of chance with. If she was carrying his baby…

'Tell me what your future plans are for her,' he demanded.

'You and Catalina will be married long enough for the child to be born and the child's legitimacy to be unquestioned. A year should do it. Then you will divorce and Catalina will publicly repent a hasty marriage with a worthless piece of scum. Your marriage won't just legitimise the child it will legitimise *her* and allow us to find a suitable husband for her.'

'You'll marry her off again?' He shook his head, incredulous that the King and his heir would go to such lengths. 'She really is nothing but a possession to you.'

A smug look settled on Dominic's face. 'Catalina is in agreement with this. She knows her place and her position.'

Speaking through gritted teeth, Nathaniel said, 'If I agree to this I want full rights to the child.'

'You forget who is in control here.'

Nathaniel leaned forward and stared hard at the Prince. 'I can walk out of this building and onto my jet and you'll never see me again, and there is nothing you or your henchman can do about it.'

Dominic swallowed.

Nathaniel bit back a smile of contempt. For all his swagger and cruelty, the Prince was as hard as an overset blancmange. Inches shorter than him, Dominic had turned soft and flabby over the years. He would probably hit the twenty-stone mark before he hit the age of forty. His henchman was muscular and used to throwing his weight around but Nathaniel would bet his fortune the bodyguard wasn't used to the fight being brought to him.

'If Catalina confirms your claims then I will marry her, but only if my rights as a father are guaranteed and as long as you understand I will not spend one night under the roof of your palace.'

If she was pregnant—and he had no reason to think Dominic was lying; it was too fantastical for the Neanderthal to dream up—then he was going to be a father.

Now the whole of Dominic's face contorted. 'On that we are in agreement. You think we want scum like you living in the Royal Palace of Monte Cleure? While you two are married, Catalina will live with you. You can both consider it an additional punishment.'

Knowing that to spend another minute with Dominic would result in him smashing his fist into the Prince's face, Nathaniel got to his feet. 'Tell your father I will come to the palace this evening to discuss things… On second thought…' He pulled out his phone and held it up. 'I will tell him myself. Now if you'll excuse me, I have a bed to fall into. Please, see yourselves out.'

And with that, he headed off to his sleeping quarters, smiling grimly when he heard the front door slam shut.

The smile lasted seconds.

The pounding in his head seemed to have turned into a pneumatic drill.

* * *

Catalina sat in the private family drawing room, drumming her nails against the hardwood of the armchair and staring blankly at the walls. She'd been sitting there, as ordered by her father, for over two hours.

Her father's anger at the situation, although less violent than her brother's reaction, had been fearsome to behold. After twenty-five years of impeccable behaviour, the perfect daughter had blown the engagement he'd spent decades engineering. Then, having been found another suitable husband, she'd promptly added to the humiliation by getting pregnant by a notorious womanising commoner. Her apologies for the shame she'd brought on the family had fallen on deaf ears. She doubted he would ever forgive her.

'You'll have to marry him,' he'd said coldly. 'That's the only way we'll be able to mitigate the negative publicity of you getting pregnant like a common whore. And you will not refuse. You will marry that piece of garbage and legitimise the bastard growing in you.'

She'd stood there, taking the abuse, refusing to show any emotion but inside she'd screamed.

Her child was not a bastard. Her child was innocent.

And Nathaniel might be a womaniser but he wasn't garbage. He'd worked for his fortune, not had it handed to him by an accident of birth.

The Christmas festivities had gone ahead as planned but the atmosphere had been toxic. She didn't doubt the entire palace knew of her situation, most likely thanks to Marion, who'd spent Christmas dinner throwing her faux sympathetic glances. As if she didn't know Marion, who thrived on secrets and intrigue and loved to spy, had been the one to tell her brother.

Catalina's hopes that a good night's sleep would soften her father's attitude had been dispelled when he'd dispatched Lauren, his private secretary, to her rooms that afternoon. Lauren had informed her she was to dine alone with only Marion for company in the family room and then wait there until further notice.

Dominic had well and truly poisoned their father's mind against her. It gave no satisfaction that it had taken twenty-five years for him to achieve this feat.

Marion's spying and sneaking skills had come into their own. She'd abandoned her post for twenty minutes, returning to inform her that Nathaniel had arrived at the palace and was in a meeting with her father.

That had been an hour ago.

Her initial jolt of excitement had long since dissolved. Her nerves were balanced as if on a tightrope, the time dragging on so long it was a relief when Dominic finally entered the room.

'Marion, leave us,' he said without any preamble.

Catalina knew their cousin would hover by the door in the hope of catching wind of something juicy to spread around the palace.

'He's agreed to marry you,' he said, standing over her with folded arms and a smug expression that didn't quite hide the fury in his eyes.

She knew perfectly well that if her fate had been left to Dominic, she would have been banished in disgrace.

If she'd got pregnant by anyone other than Nathaniel things would be a lot different. Dominic loathed Catalina, but Nathaniel was his nemesis.

'You will marry in a fortnight. They're finalising the details as we speak.'

She didn't answer. Her involvement and consent were not relevant in this situation. Her consent was rarely required for any situation. All the same...

Her lungs expanded properly for the first time in two days. Nathaniel's consent was not something she'd taken for granted. Nathaniel was a lone wolf with an aversion to relationships and not a man to be intimidated by anyone, not even a king. That he'd accepted responsibility and agreed to marry her...

Little whispers of excitement skittered over her skin, her heart thundering hard beneath her ribs.

She was going to marry Nathaniel.

Never in her wildest dreams had she allowed herself to imagine such a thing. In all the years she'd known him he'd been part of her social circle but somewhat apart, a commoner to be welcomed graciously but kept at arm's length. He'd always been considered far beneath what her family expected of her.

Her entire life had been geared towards ensnaring one of the Kalliakis Princes, men equal to her station. That Nathaniel was the only man she'd ever found physically attractive had been something she'd hardly dared acknowledge to herself.

Making love to him had been beyond her wildest dreams.

Her veins heated just to think of his touch, and turned

into a furnace as she finally allowed herself to imagine what it would be like to share a bed with him again.

'The lawyers are on their way,' Dominic continued, looking at his watch, oblivious to her private thoughts.

'What are they coming for?'

'To draw up the contract,' he answered.

Oh, yes. The contract.

'How did you get him to agree?' She couldn't hide the flicker of hope that he'd agreed without any coercion and, more than that, that he'd insisted their marriage be a real one.

She knew it was the most pathetic, flimsiest of hopes even before Dominic flashed her his cruel smile; the same smile he'd given when he'd told Catalina her pet dog had died. 'Ah, pretty Catalina is imagining a marriage of fluffy clouds and pink icing. Although I *hate* to destroy your dreams, be in no doubt this is a business decision by Giroud—I told him he would be expelled from Monte Cleure and his business development confiscated unless he married you.'

The effect of his words was as if ice had been thrown at her.

'So you did have to blackmail him.'

'You thought he would *want* to marry you?' He laughed. 'He was only happy to agree once he'd been assured the marriage would only last a year.'

Before he could continue, a secretary appeared at the door, informing them Nathaniel had finished speaking with their father and was on his way to them.

Dominic cast Catalina his vindictive smile one last time. 'He doesn't want to marry you, pretty Catalina.

He doesn't care that you will remarry immediately after your marriage is dissolved. He has no interest in your baby. All he cares about are his business interests. You must think of it as a business arrangement too. Your end of the deal is to uphold the honour of the House of Fernandez.'

She held her brother's gaze for long seconds before inclining her head sharply. 'I will remember.'

'Good. Now is your chance to begin your redemption.' His gaze turned to the door. Catalina's stomach performed a somersault to see Nathaniel stride in as if their private quarters were rooms he'd visited on many occasions.

'Nice place you've got here,' he said, looking around the luxurious living quarters with a distinctly mocking eye.

If she didn't have so many contradictory emotions raging through her, Catalina would have found his irreverence funny. Gasps of appreciation were the usual response when people entered their private rooms for the first time.

Knots formed tight in her stomach as she gazed at the one man who had seen her naked. Her heart seemed to have gained a life of its own and the palms of her hands grew damp.

He didn't look at her. His focus was on her brother, who he towered over. 'You may leave us.'

If she hadn't been trained from birth to never show inappropriate emotion, she might very well have given a hysterical laugh. The only person she had ever heard give an order to her brother was their father, who certainly didn't use the lazy, almost dismissive tone Nathaniel had just used.

Dominic turned red. Very red. Catalina half expected steam to escape from his ears.

'I wish to speak to your sister alone,' Nathaniel said when Dominic made no attempt to leave. 'We cannot speak freely without privacy.'

'You can have five minutes.'

'Ten.'

To her amazement, Dominic pursed his lips together and stormed out of the room.

Gripping tightly to the armrest, she tried to adopt the serene, half-vacant look that had served her so well throughout her life.

Green eyes fixed on her, Nathaniel sat on the uncomfortable armchair opposite. His irreverence had left the room with her brother. All she saw was cool contemplation, although it gave her fleeting gratification to judge that he looked like a man with a serious hangover.

'So it is true. You are pregnant.' He spoke quietly, unwittingly repeating the words her brother had used the day before.

Had it really only been yesterday? They had to count as the longest few days of her life, and it wasn't over yet.

'Can you tell?'

He gave a quick, rueful smile. 'There is something different about you. If I didn't know you were expecting I would assume you were ill.' He blinked a couple of times and refocused on her. '*Are* you ill?'

'Not particularly. A little sickness, that's all.'

'Is that why you missed Helios and Amy's Coronation?'

'I thought I had a stomach bug.'

He rocked his head forward and grimaced. 'When is the baby due?'

'The doctor thinks the end of August. A scan will determine it with more certainty.'

'And you are happy to marry me?'

'My happiness is irrelevant,' she answered coolly. 'Besides, it will only be for a year.'

'And you are in agreement with your father's plan for you to remarry once we've divorced?'

'I will accept whatever is good for my family and the House of Fernandez.'

Nathaniel studied her carefully, looking for a chink in the elegantly worn armour. There was nothing to be found. The passionate woman who'd come out of her shell for one glorious night had gone. The Princess he had known from a distance for many years had returned, her mask back in place. This was a woman raised to do her duty and who fully believed in it too.

Whatever Catalina felt on a personal level about the pregnancy and their situation as a whole she was keeping to herself.

If he didn't still have such vivid memories of the night they had created this mess he could believe she was a wind-up porcelain doll. But he knew there was so much more to her than this façade. He'd kissed her most intimate area and had felt the shudders that had taken her over. He could still feel her fingertips on his scalp.

He shook the memories away.

If this was the way she wanted to play things, then all to the good. This situation was beyond either of their control. Keeping things professional was the best way to proceed.

Resting his elbows on his thighs, he leaned forwards. For her part, Catalina, dressed in tight white trousers and a dusky pink silk blouse, was sitting straight with her legs gracefully crossed. Her thick raven hair had been tied into a tight bun at the nape of her neck. The last time he'd seen her it had been loose, falling almost to the base of her spine. He'd gathered it in his hands and buried his face in it...

As the day had gone on and the initial shock had dissolved with it, he'd come to the conclusion that, regardless of Dominic's threats, marrying Catalina was the right thing to do. For a start, it would give him proper rights to their child. Meeting the King, Catalina's father, had only confirmed these feelings.

The King was a formidable man whose only concern was the reputation of the House of Fernandez and as far as he was concerned this was an exercise in damage limitation. Nathaniel might be a hugely successful businessman with more money than he could ever spend, but the King ruled an entire country. Even with all the resources Nathaniel had at his disposal, the odds of him gaining any custody in this country without marriage would not be in his favour. Marrying Catalina guaranteed him cast-iron legal rights to their child.

'When we part I will make it abundantly clear that you are blameless.' That much he could do for her. 'I will do everything in my power to ensure your reputation is not damaged. We can play our parting for all its worth so the whole world's sympathy will be with you.'

'That's very kind of you,' she said with a tight smile. 'But what about your reputation?'

He shrugged. 'My personal reputation is already ruined. And I'm not a princess. Our marriage will be as quick and as painless as possible.' Although not quick enough for his liking.

He'd known from the age of seven that he had to look after himself. A decade later he'd been cast aside by his only living relative and he'd been on his own ever since. He liked it that way. He didn't have to worry about hurting people, or worry what effect his actions would have on someone else.

He liked being single and never stayed with a woman long enough for emotional ties to form.

His marriage to Catalina would be like a business relationship. He would not allow it to be anything more.

She gave a stiff nod. 'I'm sorry you're being forced into this.'

He shrugged again. 'We both are.'

'I will be doing my duty,' she pointed out, 'but I understand Dominic threatened to expel you from the country unless you agreed, and threatened to confiscate your development. That's very different.'

'Your brother made his position very clear, just as I made mine.' As Nathaniel spoke he watched her closely. Judging by her demeanour, there was nothing to suggest Catalina had any knowledge of her father and brother's threat to cut her and the baby off. It was better she didn't know, he decided. It was too cruel and too personal a threat from her own flesh and blood, and not something that would ever come to fruition, not now that he'd agreed to the marriage. Catalina and their baby would be safe.

A glimmer of a smile played on her pretty lips but the hint of sadness surrounding it negated any humour. 'My brother takes his role as heir and protector of the House of Fernandez very seriously.'

He cleared his throat, biting back the retort on his lips. Whatever his personal feelings towards Dominic, he was her brother and her loyalty would lie with him. 'Getting back to the business at hand, I want to be clear that you're in agreement to everything your father's demanding.'

'Yes. I am in agreement.'

'Then it is done.' He got to his feet. 'I need to make a move.'

Her remarkable chocolate eyes were fixed on him. 'Already?'

He didn't like the tinge of disappointment in her voice. 'I have somewhere to be.'

Dominic chose that moment to come barrelling into the room. 'You've had your ten minutes.'

Nathaniel noticed the way Catalina withdrew into herself at Dominic's return, how her lips tightened in the most subtle of fashions.

He remembered the malice on Dominic's face when he'd threatened to make Catalina homeless and penniless. The Prince was the least deserving person of his title he could think of.

'This really *is* my cue to leave.' He had no wish to spend another minute in the palace. This family room was as plush as anywhere he'd been, lavishly adorned with antique furniture and portraits dating back centuries. But there was nothing homely about it, not even with the enormous Christmas tree sitting in the corner. This room, as with the rest of the sprawling stone palace, was cold.

'Father will be hosting a select party for you two on Saturday,' Dominic said. 'My people have made contact with *La Belle* magazine—'

Nathaniel cut him off before he could speak any further. 'Tell your father he's welcome to host a party but I will not be there and I will *not* be speaking with any magazine.'

'He has already—'

'Let me make this very clear—I will not be a part of the House of Fernandez circus. I will marry your sister to legitimise our child and formalise my legal rights to it, but that is the end of my obligation. I don't want a title or anything else from your family.' He nodded at Catalina, who appeared to be frozen in her seat. 'I'll see you at the wedding.'

CHAPTER THREE

'TRY HIM AGAIN.' Catalina dug her nails into the palms of her hands, the only outward display of her inward disquiet. 'Ask him if he's free on Thursday.'

She'd asked Aliana to call Nathaniel and request a dinner date for Wednesday. He had politely declined, citing a prior engagement.

Aliana disappeared into the adjoining small office, leaving Catalina alone with Marion, whose sharp little eyes were studying her with unabashed curiosity.

'I would like you to take one of the palace cars and go to Madame Marcelle's shop and bring me back a selection of her laces.' She didn't give a reason. She didn't have a reason. All she wanted was to get rid of her cousin for a time.

'I can call and have it brought to the palace.'

'No. I wish for you to go personally. You know my tastes so I know you will choose wisely,' she added, playing to Marion's ego.

Unable to refuse, Marion nonetheless made a great show of searching for her handbag, which was at the foot of her chair.

As soon as she'd gone, Catalina breathed out and closed her eyes. Marion's behaviour, including all those sly smiles and blatant eavesdropping, had become intolerable. Or was it that the limits of her own patience had finally been reached? The pregnancy hormones were certainly rampaging through her. It was becoming a struggle to keep the poise she'd held throughout her life.

Aliana reappeared, shaking her head. 'He has a prior appointment Thursday night too.'

'And probably Friday and Saturday night,' Catalina muttered, thinking quickly. It had taken all of her courage to ask for Nathaniel's private number from her father but he had surprised her by handing it over. He hadn't looked at her though. He hadn't looked her in the eye since he'd called the life growing inside her a bastard.

It had been five days since their worlds had imploded. Since Nathaniel's visit to the palace and his agreement to the marriage, there had been only silence.

She'd spent the intervening days getting her head clear. She'd pushed aside the fleeting romantic notions she'd had, those few moments when she'd seen a future that could possibly be happy.

She didn't even know where those notions had come from. She didn't expect or want love. Love was a kind of witchcraft, a power strong enough to destroy the person suffering from it. A marriage built on mutual respect was the most she had ever hoped for, although hopes were an indulgence she rarely allowed herself.

Nathaniel was a commitment-shy womaniser of the highest order. Their brief marriage would be over before it had begun and she would remarry. Now all she cared about was the welfare of the tiny life she carried. She needed to protect it, but all she sensed was danger.

She took a long breath and straightened her spine. She would call him herself. Let him make his excuses not to see her personally.

Before she could move to her office, she rushed to the bathroom and brought up her breakfast.

Nathaniel's phone vibrated noisily on the desk.

Swearing, he cursed himself for not turning the vibration facility off when he'd switched it to silent.

The same number from ten minutes ago flashed at him.

He snatched it up, pressed the answer button and put the phone to his ear. 'Tell the Princess I am unavailable until the day of our wedding and if she doesn't like it she can—'

'It's Catalina.'

The unexpectedness of her voice and the coolness of her tone momentarily froze him.

'Are you there?' she asked. He could imagine her sitting at the round French mahogany table of the family room, legs crossed, back straight, as composed as she always was.

He cleared his throat. 'Yes, I'm here. What can I do for you?'

'I need to see you.'

'As I explained to your companion, I don't have any free time until the day of our wedding.'

'I'm sure you can make the time.'

'Is it important?'

'Nathaniel, we're having a baby together.'

'I am aware of that. It's the reason I'm marrying you.'

There was a slight pause before she said, 'Our marriage might only be temporary but our child is for life. Unless Dominic was telling me the truth and you have no interest in our child?'

He sighed. It didn't surprise him that Dominic would tell such a lie. 'He must have his wires crossed. I will want to play an active part.'

'Then show me the courtesy of meeting with me.'

There was something in her voice that gave him pause.

'If I agree then I want it to be somewhere neutral and not in the palace,' he said slowly. If he never had to set foot in that palace again he would die a happy man.

'I was going to suggest the same thing.' There was definite relief in her words. She went silent again before asking, 'Do you like opera?'

'No.'

'Good. My family have a private box at the Monte Cleure Royal Theatre. There's a production of *La Bohème* on this week. Our box is free on Friday so we can have it to ourselves.'

'I just told you, I don't like opera.'

'Then you won't find the singing a distraction when we talk.'

Rebuffing Catalina's assistant was a lot easier than rebuffing his fiancée personally. It would be easier if she were issuing hysterical orders but her sheer calmness made him feel foolish for his previous avoidance.

He knew beyond doubt that the less interaction they had as a couple, the better it would be for them both. But especially for her.

'Okay then, Friday,' he agreed, before terminating the call.

He rubbed the nape of his neck and closed his eyes.

The theatre manager greeted her personally, hurrying Catalina through a private side door and up the red-carpeted staircase to the House of Fernandez's private box before the general public had time to notice her appearance.

They'd arranged to meet in the royal box at eight p.m. She was fifteen minutes early.

To make the time pass quicker and in an attempt to smother the nerves swirling in her gut, she tucked herself into the corner and opened the programme. She had made it to the section describing the careers of the secondary players when Nathaniel slipped into the box, all six foot plus of him, looking dashingly handsome in a black tuxedo and bow tie, with a tumbler of Scotch in hand.

He was exactly on time.

Her heart battering against her ribcage, she got to her feet and gave him her hand. Dutifully, he put it to his mouth and razed his lips across her gloved knuckles. The heat from his breath sank through the satin.

'You're looking well,' he said, stepping back and openly appraising her.

'Thank you.'

'No sickness?'

'Not right now. It comes and goes.'

He gave a half-smile. 'That must be difficult.'

'I've been told it comes with the territory.'

Below them, the theatre was filling, the buzzing sound of pleasant chatter filling the air. The royal box had been specially designed for privacy, the curvature of the balcony allowing the occupants an unhindered view of the stage while protecting them, along with clever lighting, from prying eyes.

'How long does this go on for?' he asked as they took their seats.

'About three hours including intervals.'

He didn't bother hiding his grimace. 'Have you seen this before?'

'Oh, yes, it's a beautiful story and perfect for the Christmas period.' She looked at him and arched a brow, smothering the churn in her stomach at his obvious wish to be elsewhere. 'Even if opera's not your thing, I'm sure you can cope with my company for three hours. After all, you seemed happy with my company at Helios and Amy's wedding. Or has the thrill gone now that you've slept with me?'

He ran his fingers through his hair, mussing it up in the same manner he had moments before he'd placed his lips against hers for the last time.

'At this moment, the only thing I'm not happy about is spending three hours listening to ear-splitting wails being passed off as singing. I give you no guarantee I'll stay until the end.'

'So you don't deny you have no interest in my company at all?' She kept her voice even but the humiliation burned.

They were only supposed to have been for one night. They had both made that clear. No ties, no regrets. Catalina had imagined hugging their secret night close to her heart for the rest of her life and, as vain a hope as she now knew it to be, she'd imagined it would be the same for him too.

She'd thought—wished—that he would see the one positive of their marriage as being able to share a bed again.

She'd overestimated his boredom threshold.

'You're a beautiful, interesting woman. I doubt there's a man alive who wouldn't want to be in your company.'

'But you're not one of them.'

Nathaniel finally allowed himself to look at her properly. It was at moments like this that Catalina's royal upbringing became transparent. There was a directness in her speech that, while not arrogant, was certainly assured. It was clear she was used to having direct questions answered. She was always beautiful, but tonight she looked stunning in a shoulderless figure-hugging long black satin dress with matching elbow-length gloves. Her raven hair had been curled and pulled into a chignon, long ringlets loosened to frame her porcelain face.

'It was thinking with the anatomy below my waist and not my head that's got us into this trouble. Now, why don't you tell me what's on your mind?'

A range of emotions flickered over her sweet, heart-shaped face but she held his gaze.

He truly would have to be dead from the waist down not to desire her. There had hardly been a moment since he'd left her room in the Agon palace when he hadn't thought of her.

When they'd made love that night, she'd been a virgin. He'd taken things slowly, gently coaxing her eager responses. As a married couple, even with the imposed time limit, they would have all the time in the world to explore each other's desires. To imagine peeling that dress off and discovering all her secret, hedonistic fantasies...

He couldn't act on it.

Catalina was a princess, and that shone through her every word and deed. He should never have seduced her in the first place.

He'd impregnated her and caused a potentially terminal rift in her family. Further proof, as if it were needed, that he was rotten to his core. He would not allow himself to cause any more damage.

'I suggested we meet here because I needed to be sure that we can speak freely,' she said.

'You don't think that's possible in the palace?'

'I know it isn't. There's not a telephone conversation within the palace walls that isn't recorded. My father and Dominic have spies everywhere.'

'What are you worried about them hearing?'

Before she could answer, the theatre lights dimmed and the orchestra, set low in the pit before the stage, struck up. Then the curtains were drawn back and the production began.

Catalina waited until it had started in earnest before answering. Nathaniel was forced to lean in close to hear her above the noise, inhaling that irresistible scent in the process.

It was her scent that had captured his attention to begin with.

When he'd first met Catalina at a society party in France a number of years ago, her choice of perfume when he'd leaned in for the polite kisses on the cheek had intrigued him. She was the quintessential Princess, always dressed impeccably, graceful and elegant in both speech and manner. He would have expected a light floral perfume, something girlish and rather innocent. Yet she wore a sultry scent that evoked thoughts of long hot nights and dusky mornings.

He'd made love to her knowing she was a virgin. Again, she had confounded his expectations. He'd assumed she would be shy. She had been the opposite.

The demure woman sitting so elegantly beside him had a fire in her soul that had set him ablaze. Unless he was willing to risk them both being burnt, he would never touch her again.

'I wanted to speak freely because I am concerned for your safety.'

'What are you talking about?'

'My brother has a pathological loathing of you.'

'I am aware of that. He's never liked me. Trust me, the feeling is mutual but I would never wish to harm him.' Nathaniel grimaced. 'Sorry, that was a lie. I admit, there have been numerous occasions when I would have liked to give him a good hiding.'

Her lips twitched. She put a hand to her mouth and

cleared her throat. 'Forgive me for asking, but what happened between you at school? Dominic never went into detail but I remember him coming home for the Christmas holidays when I was a child crowing that you'd been expelled.'

His mouth pursed and he shook his head. 'We fell out over a girl.'

'What happened?'

'He caught me in bed with his girlfriend at our school Christmas party.'

She gave a surprised bark of laughter. 'You slept with his girlfriend?'

'I wouldn't go so far as to call it sleeping but we were in a state of undress, yes.'

'Did you know she was his girlfriend?'

'Yes.'

'Did you target her deliberately?'

'No. We were both drunk and she came on to me.'

He didn't look at her, not wanting to see the disgust and disapproval bound to be on her face.

'Dominic said you only slept with me to get one up on him. Is that true?'

'No.' He shook his head emphatically. 'I admit, you being his sister gave it an extra frisson but I wanted you regardless.'

She contemplated him in silence for a while, her porcelain mask still in place.

'Your brother has hated me since we were eight,' he said. 'I have no idea what triggered it but trust me when I say the loathing was—is—mutual. We had more than our share of fights during our school years but, whatever you might think of me, I would never have seduced you to hurt him. I slept with you because the opportunity was there and I'd wanted you for years.'

Her head rocked forward. 'Thank you for being honest with me, brutal though the truth is.'

'I was honest with you from the start.'

Her gaze didn't falter but her face screwed up a little with concentration, as if she were deciding whether to share what she was thinking. Eventually she gave a sharp nod and said, 'My father sent Dominic to the same boarding school as the Kalliakis Princes specifically to cultivate a friendship with them and strengthen the ties between our two nations.'

'Your brother knew this was why he was sent there?'

'Of course.' She gave a surprising low laugh. 'I think that's why he disliked you so much. They accepted you, a commoner, as their friend—as one of them. Dominic was born of royal blood and he found himself being treated exactly the same as you, which he detested. You were supposed to know your place, not be more popular than him. If you stole his girlfriend I don't imagine that endeared you to him. And now that he knows you've...' She cleared her throat and looked away. 'That you and I...'

'Were together?' he supplied, his body tightening as he recalled the exact feeling of being inside her.

She nodded sharply. 'Dominic and I have never had the closest of sibling relationships. Couple that with his loathing of you... He would have been more accepting if Satan himself had impregnated me. If Dominic held the throne he would have thrown me out on the spot.'

Nathaniel rubbed his temples, letting her words soak into his brain. He would never tell her that her suspicions were correct, but it was much worse than she thought; that if he'd refused to marry her, she *would* have been thrown out, and the order would have come right from the top, from her father.

'I concede that Dominic has hated me for years but I don't get why you think I might be in danger from him. I've agreed to the marriage. Our child will be legitimate. And then I will walk away and leave you free to marry someone of equal nobility. He will have everything as he wants it.'

'I know he's something of a joke to you but I worry you underestimate how dangerous he can be. He is more than capable of hurting someone.'

There was something in her tone that made him look at her carefully. He'd heard rumours over the years about Dominic's free and easy hands with some of his girlfriends. Was there truth in those rumours? He recalled Catalina's reaction when her brother had come back into the room at the palace, the subtle withdrawal. 'Has he ever hurt you?'

'What a question to ask,' she said, her voice light.

'And what a non-answer to give.'

Her head tilted slightly but she kept her gaze on the stage where the opera was in full flow. 'All siblings argue. I might be making something out of nothing but, in Dominic's eyes, you've humiliated him. He is not a man to mess with.'

'And neither am I. Trust me, if your brother attempts

anything against me or my business interests, he will regret it.'

The curtains closed for the end of the first act and applause echoed through the theatre.

Spotting an opportunity, Nathaniel drained the last of his Scotch and got to his feet. 'Was there anything else you wanted to talk about?'

'You're leaving?'

'I told you, I despise opera.' That was only the partial truth. The full truth was that their private box was shrinking by the second, Catalina's scent seeping into all the crevices, filling his senses.

A flash of colour heightened her cheeks. 'We're getting married next week. Shouldn't we talk about that and what our marriage will entail?'

'Our marriage will entail nothing more than getting you and the baby safely through the pregnancy. I will ensure your every need is met. Now, can I offer you a lift home? Or do you want to stay and watch the rest?'

'Thank you for your generous offer,' she said, irony heavily lacing her voice, 'but I'll stay.'

'As you wish.' He bowed his head. 'I thank you for sharing your concerns with me—I know loyalty and duty to the House of Fernandez are things you believe strongly in. It can't be easy to speak of your brother like this.'

It must have taken a lot of courage for her to speak out against him. That the Prince was a bully was indisputable. How many times had he turned that nasty tongue on her? Catalina being pregnant with Nathaniel's child would surely only make his viciousness worse.

While Nathaniel didn't relish giving up his freedom, at least having Catalina under his own roof rather than in the palace would give her space away from her brother's malevolence.

And at least when she remarried she'd be far from his influence then too, and so would their child. The contract he and the King had drawn up had given Nathaniel very specific rights to his child. If the King tried to renege on it, he knew hellfire would rain down on him and his country.

She turned her head, those chocolate-brown eyes that fixed on him void of emotion. 'I know you're only marrying me because you've been blackmailed into it, but you're the father of my child and that means I owe some loyalty to you too, for our baby's sake.'

'So your personal feelings towards me...?' He deliberately let his words tail off so she could fill the silence.

Was the attraction she had held for him still there or had their night together quelled it? With any other woman he would be able to make a good judgement call, but Catalina was a princess, trained from birth to hide her emotions. Outwardly, she did not give anything away.

What would she do if he were to trace his fingers up her spine then move his hand around to cup one of those heavenly breasts? Such was the privacy the box gave them, he could lay her down and make love to her without anyone seeing...

He fully understood now why she'd been given three chaperones. She really was the most naturally sensual of women. And he needed to get out of this theatre before he did something stupid. Like seduce her all over again.

'Are non-existent.' Her mouth snapped shut and she turned her gaze back to the empty stage. 'Have a safe drive home.'

Catalina didn't breathe again until she heard the door to the box close. Only then did her lungs expand enough for her to gulp in some air.

Nathaniel couldn't have made it clearer that he considered marriage to her akin to sleeping in a tank of snakes.

Whatever secret dreams she'd had she would keep to herself. If there was one thing she had learnt throughout her life it was to keep her emotions in check. She wasn't in love with him but she wasn't going to lie to herself and pretend she didn't have feelings for him. How could she pretend when his departure made the generous box feel so empty and she could still smell his musky, citrus-like scent?

Whatever happened, she would not allow these feelings to develop further. She'd seen for herself the misery and heartbreak of denied love and had known since she was eighteen that she would never allow that for herself.

She would do as her brother ordered and treat this marriage as a business arrangement.

CHAPTER FOUR

OVERNIGHT, THE BALMY weather of the past few weeks turned into torrential rain. Even Monte Cleure, famed for its year-round sun, had to deal with winter in some form or other.

The weather hadn't been enough to deter the well-wishers however. Peering through binoculars from her bedroom window, Catalina could see them lining the palace perimeter, huddled under umbrellas.

The people of Monte Cleure clearly hadn't taken the palace's statement that today's wedding would be a 'small, private affair' to heart.

It touched her to see them there and it warmed her too.

This was what she was doing it for. These people without whose good wishes and consent her family would have nothing. Her father ruled but, as with all monarchies in this day and age, his grip was not as firm as it had once been. If the people revolted, he could do nothing to turn the tide.

In order for the House of Fernandez to endure, it had to bring peace and prosperity to its people. The House of Fernandez had to be loved. And it had to be above reproach. Dominic's lusty antics were tolerated with ironic smiles; his public persona very much at odds with the private man behind closed doors. When he finally took the plunge and married, the whole country would unite as one to celebrate. Catalina hoped he put the day off for as long as possible. She couldn't bear to think of how he would treat his wife.

But now was not the time to worry about her hypothetical future sister-in-law. She had her own wedding to get through. In three hours she would marry Nathaniel. Tonight she would move into his apartment.

The thought of living with him…it should terrify her. But the bubbles in her stomach didn't feel like terror. They felt more like excitement. They would be a married couple. And that meant sharing a bed…

She hated the excitement she felt at that. He'd made his disinterest abundantly clear during their night at the opera a week ago. Not only had he spelt it out in so many words, he'd then compounded it by leaving her in the first interval. She hadn't seen anything of him since. He hadn't taken her out or asked to see her or even called.

There was a knock on her bedroom door. Marion, naturally hanging around like a bad smell, went to open it.

Expecting to see her other companions, ready to start preparations to beautify Catalina for the main event, she was surprised to find her father's private secretary, Lauren, standing there. Behind her stood four of her father's more junior assistants.

'Excuse me for disturbing you, Your Highness,' Lauren said, 'but we need to do an inventory of your jewellery.'

'What for?'

'Your father has requested a full list of all the jewellery in your possession.'

'What for?' she repeated, wishing that Marion weren't there watching her act like such a simpleton.

'I'm not privy to his reasons. I assume it has something to do with your move.' There was no mistaking the pity in Lauren's eyes, but it didn't detract from her matter-of-fact tone. 'Your father is in his rooms if you wish to discuss it with him, but I have my orders and I need to report back in two hours. I will also need to take an inventory of your clothes.'

'I'm getting married in three hours.'

'It has to be done now. Your father will use it to decide which of your possessions will remain in the palace. He has staff in place to package the remainder during the celebrations for you.'

'Marion, get my father on the line for me,' Catalina said in a far snappier tone than she normally used.

First the press release issued the other day without any prior warning, stating that all her royal duties and patronages were being suspended 'for the foreseeable future', ostensibly to allow her time to settle into her new marriage, and now this?

What punishment would her father inflict next? Would he force her to strip to her underwear and do the walk of shame like her ancestors had done in medieval times?

From the look on her cousin's face, Marion was as

much in the dark as she was. That was the only bright spot in this situation.

But either her father really was unavailable or he didn't want to talk to her. Marion reported back that he would see her when it was time to walk her down the aisle.

Her mind awhirl over what this all meant, Catalina forced herself to remain outwardly calm. There was nothing she could do about any of it at that moment.

But when an excited Aliana and Louisa arrived, and Catalina was sitting at her dresser as they began their work, she couldn't switch off her mind.

Was it really such a shameful thing she had done? After all, Isabella, her younger sister, had been allowed to marry non-royalty. Their father had even given his blessing. But then, Isabella's husband, although he was a commoner too, didn't have Nathaniel's lousy reputation.

And Isabella had always been able to twist both their father and Dominic around her little finger.

Catalina had always been the good, dutiful daughter but now one mistake had turned her into an outcast.

Make that two mistakes. She'd let Helios go. In her father's eyes, their broken engagement was her fault and the subsequent perceived shame heaped on the House of Fernandez her fault too. In his eyes, she hadn't tried hard enough to keep him. The daughter he had groomed to marry one of the Kalliakis Princes—and any of them would have done—had let them all slip through her fingers, destroying the Great Marriage he had engineered from the day of her birth.

Isabella was lucky she had fallen in love with Sebastien before any of the Kalliakis Princes had married, Catalina thought ruefully. Their father had given his blessing to his favourite daughter, arrogantly assuming Catalina would snare the greatest prize.

As serene as she tried to appear to be, as she sat there with her companions fussing over her, applying her make-up and doing her hair, it felt like nails scraping down a blackboard to witness Lauren and her assistants trawl through her wardrobes and jewellery boxes, carefully and efficiently itemising each and every single one of her possessions. One of them even made a note of the earrings she had on.

Nothing felt right. She'd left the opera with little peace, and the disquiet within her had grown as the days had passed. She was marrying Nathaniel for the sake of her family. All her life she had put duty above her own feelings. Always, she had accepted that was the way things were. But for the first time, she wanted to rail against it. The serenity with which she had endured her life had dissolved and now bubbled in her veins like carbonated lava.

Knowing Nathaniel was only marrying her to protect his investment…it sent those bubbles into a frenzy. It was the polar opposite of the way she'd felt while engaged to Helios, who had only intended to marry her for the blueness of her blood and the heir she was supposed to provide. Whoever she married after Nathaniel would also expect an heir.

Somehow being regarded as a blue-blooded breeding machine didn't evoke a fraction of the anger the thought of marrying Nathaniel did.

Marrying Nathaniel...

She had never felt so many heightened emotions in her life.

She had never been more *scared* in her life.

She was also scared for her future. How would Johann, the Swedish duke, or whoever she was forced to marry after Nathaniel, treat her child? How would they treat *her*?

'I bet you wish your mother was here to see this,' Marion observed in a faux sympathetic voice in the moments before they were due to leave Catalina's rooms. Aliana, who was straightening the tiara, glared at her. Marion was not a popular member of the household.

Catalina met her cousin's reflection in the mirror, unwittingly scrunching the ivory satin skirt of her dress between her fingers.

She had done everything in her power not to think of her mother that day. Marion would have been kinder if she'd plunged a knife into her back.

Tilting her chin up, Catalina said coldly, 'Thank you for reminding me of what I'm missing out on. Your support today has been invaluable.'

While her cousin stood there frowning, clearly unsure whether Catalina had just paid her a compliment or put her down, Catalina took Aliana's hand and got to her feet.

If her mother were alive it would have been her hand she'd be holding for support. Her mother had been the one person Catalina had never had to put the mask on for.

She blinked rapidly to rid herself of the unexpected

tears welling in her eyes and placed a hand to her stomach.

If her mother were alive everything would still be the same as it was now. Her mother had always put the House of Fernandez first. Duty above desire. Duty above love. Catalina would still be expected to hold her head up high and do her duty.

But if her mother were still alive she would be able to hold her hand while she did it.

Even for this supposedly small and private wedding, around one hundred guests were crammed in the Monte Cleure Palace Chapel. Nathaniel was quite certain that if Catalina were marrying a fellow aristocrat, the ceremony would take place in her country's famed cathedral with fellow royalty and world leaders as guests. It would be a full weekend of celebrations, not the short service followed by the palace banquet they would shortly be having.

For anyone else, today's events would seem a wedding to be proud of. For Catalina, it would be seen as another punishment.

He had to hand it to the King—he was playing an excellent hand. A wedding such as this showed the world his support for his daughter but also his subtle disapproval of his new son-in-law. When the marriage was dissolved a year from now, the King would be perceived as a wise, loving father who had put his daughter's happiness above his own doubts.

What would the King do, Nathaniel wondered idly, if he refused to divorce her? What would *Dominic* do?

Imagining their apoplectic rage amused him for a few seconds before he dismissed the notion.

Whatever his personal feelings towards the House of Fernandez, this was Catalina's life and she was a willing participant in her family's future plans for her. He'd screwed her life up enough without destroying it completely, and he'd already destroyed enough lives for any person to have on their conscience.

His job, as he saw it, was to get Catalina through the pregnancy, keeping both her and the baby safe. Nothing more. And if the vivid memory of being inside her didn't fade away, he would just have to live with it.

It had pleased him to see the crowds of people lining the palace's perimeter. At least her people loved her. And so they should. Catalina was an excellent ambassador for her country, celebrated the world over for her ethereal loveliness and gracious manner of dealing with people.

While he recognised most of the guests in attendance, he personally knew only a handful, which suited him perfectly. Who wanted to make false vows in front of people who really mattered? Not him.

Not that there was anyone left in his life who did matter.

He tried to imagine the child forming in Catalina's womb. *His* child. A fragile life that would need his love and protection. The vows he was about to make would enable that.

In the back of the chapel, a photographer fiddled with his camera's tripod. *La Belle* magazine was publishing a special wedding edition documenting the day.

Nathaniel had made it clear that he would not be involved with it in any regard other than the official photographs.

'Not long now,' Sebastien Duchamp murmured beside him.

Sebastien, a security expert, had married Catalina's younger sister Isabella earlier the previous year and was acting as Nathaniel's best man. The King had insisted that he have one. As Nathaniel had already won a number of significant victories over the King and his heir, on this one point he had been prepared to concede ground. Sebastien had seemed as good a choice as any, and Nathaniel didn't need to lie to him. Being a member of the House of Fernandez—albeit in a peripheral sense—he knew exactly why the marriage was taking place.

As he turned to look at Dominic, Nathaniel caught the malevolence on the Prince's face and was again reminded of Catalina's warning. For all his outward dismissal of the threat, he had thought it prudent to increase his security and had employed Sebastien the day after the torturous opera visit to do a thorough check of his Monte Cleure home and business premises for any potential weaknesses. Sebastien had declared it all in good order.

On a personal level, there was little Nathaniel detested more than the sight of fully grown men parading themselves with a gaggle of bodyguards in tow. It was nothing more than a status symbol. They might as well have signs on their heads reading 'Man of wealth. Come and get me.' However, with Catalina moving in with him and her father truculently refusing to allow her previous bodyguards to move with her, Nathaniel had employed four of Sebastien's men for the duration of their marriage and extra security for his apartment building.

Nathaniel might not be deemed good enough for the King's daughter but his money was deemed good enough to keep her.

He checked his watch.

Two minutes to go. With any luck, this would all be over within the hour.

Although it was fashionable for a bride to be late, he'd made a bet with himself that Catalina would arrive at the chapel exactly on time.

A tall man with the shiniest bald head he'd ever seen hurried into the church, taking a seat in the back row. Nathaniel had to bite the inside of his cheek to hide his amusement. Did the man polish his pate? Hot on his heels was a woman wearing a bright pink dress and a matching hat wide enough to hit the lady in the seat in front of her.

Then, right on cue, Catalina arrived.

The guests rose to their feet as one, craning their necks for the first glimpse of the bride.

As she stepped over the threshold, her right hand enfolded in her father's arm, Nathaniel found a lump forming in his throat that no amount of swallowing could dislodge. All his amusement, cynicism and detachment vanished.

The rain outside had turned into a full-blown storm in the time he'd been in the chapel and gusts blew at the train of her ivory dress, which had a rounded neckline that skimmed her creamy breasts and tapered to her waist. It was as if she had a wind machine behind her.

A veil covered her face but as she walked slowly up the aisle it struck him that she resembled a walking statue. Nothing in her body language suggested any kind of emotion. The only person with less animation was the King. If her father's jaw clenched any tighter Nathaniel was sure his face would crack.

When she reached his side, the King took a step back, not even deigning to look at Nathaniel.

With a tightness inside he hadn't felt in decades, he lifted her veil.

She wasn't quick enough to hide the truth he saw in her eyes.

Catalina was *furious*.

Then she blinked and the fury vanished, leaving only the porcelain mask of her beautiful face.

When it was her turn to recite their vows, her voice was nothing but a flat monotone.

Catalina picked at her food without appetite. They were on the dessert course of *mille-feuille* and she couldn't even remember what had been served for any of the other courses. She couldn't blame it on the morning sickness. Ironically, today was the first day in weeks she hadn't felt nauseous. Her stomach was too empty to feel anything.

Their wedding feast was being held in the smallest of the palace staterooms. She was surprised her father and brother hadn't held it in one of the greenhouses.

She hadn't had the chance to question her father

about the inventory. He'd deliberately waited until the last minute to join her at the chapel entrance and the doors had been opened for them before she'd had a chance to open her mouth.

When she contrasted it with his behaviour during Isabella's wedding, when he'd personally collected her sister from her rooms and escorted her in a horse-drawn carriage to the cathedral, his face beaming with pride...

Even Isabella, as self-absorbed as she generally was—and she'd only made it to the palace with minutes to spare—had been upset by the way Catalina had been treated. Her little sister had held her hand the whole way to the chapel.

Lucky, lucky Isabella. She'd fallen madly in love with a commoner and been allowed to marry him with both their father and brother's blessings.

Isabella and Sebastien were besotted with each other. Catalina's heart ached to see the tenderness between them; true love in all its glory. Marriages in the House of Fernandez were generally arranged like business deals and her parents' marriage had been no exception. Catalina's marriage to Helios would have been the same.

To witness with her own eyes how a true marriage could be...

It would never happen for her. She wished she hadn't seen it because now she had witnessed everything she would never have.

The affection between Isabella and Sebastien only heightened the contrast between Catalina and her new husband. Throughout the meal, conversation between her and Nathaniel had been pointedly polite.

She hadn't expected any overt displays of affection but he'd acted as if they were having an ordinary meal and she were an ordinary person he'd been sitting next to. There wasn't intimacy in his eyes when he looked at her. There was nothing there, not even the sparkle that had always resonated from them in the past.

The kiss that had sealed their vows in the chapel had been nothing but a fleeting brush of his lips against hers. It had contained less meaning than a goodnight kiss from a relative.

The ache in her heart was growing by the second. It was ridiculous. She knew the score.

'Who's here from your side?' she asked. She'd searched the faces of their guests a dozen times wondering who Nathaniel's guests were.

'No one.'

'Why?'

'Because this is a farce.'

'Yes,' she agreed, taking a sip of orange juice. She wished it were wine. 'I just thought you might have your family here for support.' She knew he'd lost his parents at a young age but surely everyone had some family?

'There aren't many of us.' He gave a short smile and took a bite of his *mille-feuille*. Tiny flakes of pastry fell onto his chin and he wiped them away with his thumb.

His tone suggested this wasn't a conversation he wanted to take forward.

'Did you invite them?'

'No.' He stared pointedly at her full plate. 'You need to eat something.'

'I'm not hungry.' How could anyone eat with a room

full of eyes upon them? Catalina was used to her every move being scrutinised but this felt much more intrusive. Nothing had been confirmed publicly about her pregnancy, and nor would it be for a number of months, but everyone present either knew of it or suspected it.

It didn't matter what people believed.

In a few short hours she would be moving out of the only home she had ever known and into the home of a man who saw her as an encumbrance.

There would be no happy ending for either of them.

The storm had died down by the time the celebrations were over.

When Nathaniel suggested they leave shortly before eleven, Catalina smiled and got to her feet without comment.

She had performed beautifully throughout the reception; a princess in every sense of the word. Her lack of appetite had been the only outward sign of anything being amiss. That, and her eyes containing all the emotion of a porcelain doll. The only real emotion he'd seen had been that flash of fury when he'd lifted her veil.

It was impossible to know what was going on in her head.

'Are we not going to wait for my cases?' she asked when his driver turned the engine on.

'They've already been sent to my apartment.'

She gave a nod and looked out of the window.

After many minutes of silence, he said, 'Is there something on your mind, Catalina?'

She took a long, quiet breath before answering. 'My

father sent his assistant and her team into my rooms earlier to do an inventory of my possessions.'

'When you say your possessions, what are we talking about?'

'Everything. My clothes and jewellery, my books... everything. I'm concerned about the timing. It was deliberately timed for when I was preparing for our marriage. And I'm concerned about what he wants it for.'

'What do you think he's going to do with the inventory?' he asked carefully, recalling his conversation with Dominic and the Prince's threats to make Catalina homeless and penniless.

'I don't know. That's what's so frightening. It was definitely a warning of some kind. A power thing. I don't know.' She tilted her head back and closed her eyes. 'Another punishment for the situation I've put us all in.'

Nathaniel balled his hands into fists.

It infuriated him that the King allowed Dominic's prejudice to influence him so much. He quite understood why the King didn't think him good enough for his daughter—with his reputation he could hardly blame him—but to treat her in such a manner was unforgivable.

Family dynamics were a strange and complex thing but this was her own flesh and blood acting so cruelly towards her.

And then he remembered what he'd done to *his* own flesh and blood. It had been unforgivable, and no amount of repentance could ever change that.

'I'm sure you have nothing to worry about,' he lied

smoothly. When it came to her father and brother, he would put nothing past them.

From the corner of his eye he saw her chest rise, and those gloriously heavy breasts lifting with the motion. The desire he'd spent the whole day suppressing suddenly came to the fore, a stab of lust piercing him, so powerful not even the mightiest of willpower could keep it contained.

He was thrown back to when she'd lain beneath him, naked, the echo of her heartbeat pulsing through her chest.

He'd reluctantly—reluctant only because at that point he hadn't wanted to let go of her—moved to get a condom when she'd gripped his wrist. 'Do you always use protection?' she'd whispered.

'Always.'

She'd swallowed and palmed his cheek. 'If this is the only chance I get to make love with someone I desire then I want to experience all of it. I want to feel you inside me as you are.'

He'd stared into those sultry eyes a man could sink into and known she was serious. And known he wanted nothing more than to experience all of it too, as he had never wanted to before.

'Please,' she'd said, her voice so low he'd had to strain to hear it. 'Just for this one moment.'

Nathaniel had had many lovers in his life. Several had been on the pill or used other forms of contraception and had told him he didn't need the condoms. It had never been something he would even contemplate.

With Catalina…

He'd taken her that first time completely bare. He'd taken it slowly, using all his experience and willpower to stop himself from getting carried away before he'd withdrawn and sheathed himself.

The thought came into his mind that now she was his wife and their moment of wilful madness had resulted in pregnancy, he could make love to her whenever and wherever he liked and be able to feel *every* part of it.

He pushed the thought away, angry with himself for letting his mind wander in directions it shouldn't go.

This marriage was to secure his rights to his child, protect Catalina from her family's vindictiveness and protect his huge investment in this country. It could never be more than that.

The silence between them lasted until his driver parked in the underground garage beneath the building.

Right in front of his designated spaces was the private elevator, manned by a security guard.

Nathaniel punched in the code and the doors opened.

'This elevator is for our private use,' he explained as they stepped inside. 'It only goes to my apartment.'

When they reached the top floor he stood aside to let her in.

Wherever he happened to be based, Nathaniel liked to surround himself in comfort. He owned property all over the world. He wanted for nothing. He need not work another day in his life and still he would never want for anything.

Catalina, though, was a princess. She had been raised in a palace of one of the oldest, most famous families in the world. Luxury was nothing new to her. The luxury Nathaniel lived in was of a very different, more modern kind.

'This is not what I expected,' she said as she trailed him into the main living area of the large, open space. Nathaniel's apartment, with its high ceilings and tall windows, covered the entire top floor. She stared with definite interest at the expensive furniture and adornments.

'What were you expecting?'

One elegant shoulder raised into a shrug. 'Something showy. It's bigger than I thought it would be. It reminds me of those loft conversions you see in New York.'

'You've been to New York?'

A wistful smile. 'No. *La Belle* often interviews famous New Yorkers in their homes. I like to look at pictures of other people's homes.'

'You have travelled though,' he stated casually, not liking the tug her wistfulness had evoked in him.

'Extensively. After my mother died I became my father's official consort and accompanied him on many of his overseas state visits. We always stayed in official residences, never informal homes.' Both her shoulders rose this time. 'Living somewhere like this…it will be new for me.'

Like pulling a swan out of its lake and placing it in a pond.

Another tug pulled at his guts.

'I'll introduce you to Frederic,' he said. 'He will make the transition easier for you.'

Seconds later, his butler appeared. Frederic took

Catalina's hand and bowed. 'It is an honour to have you here, Your Highness.'

She gave Frederic her first genuine smile of the day. 'If I'm going to be living here, you must call me Catalina.'

He looked almost offended. 'I could never be so informal.'

'Only in private,' she said kindly. 'When there are guests you can be as formal as you wish.'

'Nicely done,' Nathaniel said when Frederic had disappeared to the staff quarters. 'You had him eating out of your hand in thirty seconds flat.'

In one short conversation, Catalina had dispelled the notion that she was some kind of mythical creature from a fairy tale and had put Frederic at his ease too.

'People are always scared when they meet me,' she replied. 'They don't think I'm human.'

'When they get to know you their preconceptions will change.'

She nodded, before asking quietly, 'Can I ask when my companions will be joining me?'

'Didn't your father tell you? Your companions are to stay at the palace.'

Her eyes widened a fraction.

'It's to minimise disruption,' he lied. 'When our marriage is over and you return to the palace, they will be ready to resume their duties. In the meantime, I have staff here who will take care of your every need.'

In actual fact, her father's words had been, 'She can live with you in your apartment but her personal staff belong to the House of Fernandez. They're not going anywhere.' Another thing Nathaniel would not be sharing with her.

'That is very kind of you.' Her voice sounded hoarse.

'You must be tired,' he said. 'Let me show you to your room. I'll introduce you to the rest of the staff in the morning.'

'I look forward to it.' Her smile didn't meet her eyes.

He extended an arm to her. 'The sleeping quarters are this way.'

Far too aware of her following in his steps, Nathaniel focused his attention on the door at the other side of the living space. Lights came on automatically when he opened it, bathing the large square hallway in warmth.

He opened the door to the right. 'This is your room. The staff have unpacked your clothes for you in your dressing room. The bathroom is fully stocked but if there's anything amiss then press the green button by the side of your bed. Frederic has agreed to stay on call for the night. If there's anything you need, anything at all, press the button and he will come.' Nathaniel deliberately kept the smooth flow of information going, far too aware that Catalina seemed to have shrunk into herself.

'Do you have everything you need?' he asked when he had shown her everything.

Her eyes darted around the room and she nodded.

He headed to the door. 'In that case, I will say goodnight.'

'Where are you going?' They were the first words she'd uttered since she'd entered the room.

'To bed. It's been a long day.'

'But…' For the first time in all the years he'd known her, real colour heightened her cheeks. 'Aren't we going to share a bed?'

'No.' The word came out much sharper than he'd intended. He dragged a hand across his jaw. 'Sleeping together would be asking for trouble.'

'But no one will believe our child was conceived within marriage if we don't share a bed.'

'The whole world already believes this was a shotgun marriage.' Seeing her eyes cloud over, he added, 'No one will know of our sleeping arrangements.'

'Your staff will.'

'They won't say a word.'

'How can you be sure?'

'They're loyal to me.'

'You trust them not to sell us out?'

'I trust them implicitly,' he stated firmly. 'As I said, they're loyal to me.'

'You must pay them a fortune for such loyalty.'

'Loyalty doesn't have a price.'

'It does in my world,' she said with a touch of sadness.

'This will be your home for the foreseeable future. You don't have to worry about spies reporting back to your father or Dominic. My staff are discreet and they will take good care of you.' He opened the door. 'Goodnight, Catalina.'

'Goodnight,' she whispered to the closing door.

CHAPTER FIVE

HOW MUCH HUMILIATION could one person take?

Catalina blinked back the tears that had been threatening all day, mortification ravaging her.

Nathaniel no longer found her attractive. Whether it was because she was pregnant or because he'd had her once and had no wish to repeat the experience, she didn't know and she didn't care. It was the final indignity to add to what had been an awful, horrendous day.

She could already imagine the headlines of the *La Belle* piece and knew that at some point the text would say the immortal words, 'best day of her life'.

And yet it had to rank as one of the worst; certainly the worst since the day she'd said goodbye to her mother.

She spun around in this strange room that was to be hers alone. There wasn't even the pretence of a real marriage. She was going to live as Nathaniel's wife for a year and he wanted nothing physical to do with her.

Being rejected by Helios had been bad enough, but this...

It was infinitely worse. She hadn't had any feelings for Helios, whereas her feelings for Nathaniel were all over the place. One minute she wanted to hit him, the next she was yearning to feel his warm, firm lips upon hers again and to rediscover the touch of his hands upon her skin.

She'd prepared herself for emotional distance between them, especially since the opera, but it had never entered her head there would be physical distance too.

A celibate marriage? To one of France's most notorious playboys?

She could only imagine Dominic's crowing if he were to discover Nathaniel found her so unattractive he wouldn't even share a bed with her.

The nausea that had been kept at bay all day suddenly hit her with a vengeance. She only just made it to her bathroom before she brought up the remnants of the little food she'd managed to eat.

Afterwards, she sat on the heated floor tiles and clutched her head. There was a buzzing in her brain making it hard for her to think straight, but think she *must*.

This apartment was her home for the next year. She couldn't spend that time sitting on the bathroom floor feeling sorry for herself. Self-pity never changed anything.

Dragging herself to her feet, she looked from the inviting freestanding bath to the walk-in shower section of the bathroom. As she debated which to take, she noticed the toiletries that had been neatly placed on the tray by the bath. They were the exact brands she used at home.

In some small way, Nathaniel was trying to make this easy and painless for her.

She took the lid off the bubble bath and sniffed, feeling better with the familiar scent in her nose. And then she caught sight of her reflection.

She wouldn't be able to have a bath or a shower if she didn't get out of her wedding dress. The only problem was how she would do that.

For a fortnight she'd let her secret thoughts dart to places she should never have allowed them to go; to a place where Nathaniel had been the one to take the dress off for her. She had imagined the scenario in detail.

Did helping her out of her wedding dress count as something Frederic was supposed to deal with? Surely not. Her companions had always been the ones to help her. She could never ask a man.

Should she ask Nathaniel?

Absolutely not. She didn't have to give him another excuse to reject her.

And just like that, the calm she'd found with the scent of the bubble bath evaporated and anger pushed its way through.

She was a fully grown woman but as helpless as a child. She'd been raised this way. It hadn't been her choice.

Well, she decided, she was going to have to learn to take care of herself. Starting right now.

Returning to the bedroom, she hunted through drawers and opened cupboards until she found what she was looking for.

She took the scissors into her hands and carefully placed them at the sleeves of her dress. And then she snipped. She snipped her dress until the fabric fell away and she could step out of it.

It felt like shedding skin.

* * *

'Are you sure this is all the stuff that was sent from the palace?' Catalina asked Clotilde, who was watching her anxiously. They were in her dressing room. It wasn't even a quarter filled.

Clotilde nodded. 'Two suitcases. Were you expecting more? It doesn't seem very much for a princess.'

Catalina pasted a smile to her face, fighting hard not to let her anxiety show. 'Thank you for helping me look. I'm sure it's just an oversight. I'll call my father and have the rest of my possessions sent on.'

Nathaniel had said she could trust his staff's discretion but he hadn't been the one who'd spent a lifetime living with spies and turncoats. Clotilde had introduced herself twenty minutes ago when she'd brought Catalina breakfast in bed, proudly informing her that she would be her dedicated companion. Her eagerness was touching.

A few years younger than herself, Clotilde was a breath of fresh air and reminded her of Aliana, her favourite of her palace companions.

But, however nice and eager to please Clotilde appeared to be, Catalina didn't know her. It was far too early to trust anyone in this household. She couldn't rule out the possibility that her father had already bought them and that every word or deed made under this roof would be reported back to him.

Clotilde nodded brightly. 'What shall I do for you now?'

'Can you show me how to use the shower?' She'd been desperate for a shower once she'd cut off her wedding dress but hadn't been able to work out how to turn it on. Now, after discovering what her father had done, she wanted nothing more than a few minutes of peace to wash it all away and gather her thoughts before the stinging behind her eyes turned into tears.

She followed Clotilde into the bathroom, where her new companion opened the shower door.

'Turn the left side for your temperature...'

'Does red indicate hot?'

She nodded. 'The right side one is the pressure.'

'And how does the bath work?'

The look Clotilde gave her made her feel like a child.

'I've never run a bath for myself or turned a shower on before,' she said quietly, wishing she didn't feel the need to explain herself.

Clotilde's eyes resembled an owl's. 'Never?'

'Never. My companions have always done everything for me.'

After showing her how to turn the taps on, Clotilde said with a theatrical sigh, 'I would love to be a princess, and be waited on all the time.'

Catalina gave a wry smile, biting back the retort that being a princess wasn't all it was made out to be. 'I've never even brushed my own hair.'

'I am very envious of your hair. Would you like me to brush it for you now?'

How hard could brushing hair be? 'I think it is time I learned how to do the basic things for myself, don't you agree?'

From the look in Clotilde's eyes, she most definitely did not agree.

'I thank you for all your assistance but I can manage on my own now.'

'I don't think Nathaniel will be pleased if I leave you to look after yourself.'

Was that because he wanted reports on her behaviour like her father had always insisted on from her palace companions?

'Then don't tell him.'

'But he said I was to stay with you at all times.'

Catalina gritted her teeth behind her smile. None of this was Clotilde's fault. Nathaniel was her employer. She was obeying orders. 'Why don't you wait in the bedroom for me?'

'You will call me if you want anything?'

'I will,' she promised. 'Thank you, Clotilde.'

Her new companion beamed as she closed the bathroom door behind her.

Alone for the first time since she'd awoken that morning, Catalina closed her eyes and wished away the tears still gathering behind her lids.

She'd had three dedicated rooms in the palace. How could all that have been reduced to two suitcases of basic everyday clothing? Everything of sentimental or monetary value had been left behind. Her portion of her mother's jewellery...

She could understand why her father had kept the heirlooms that had been passed down through the House of Fernandez, although it would have been nice if he'd mentioned his intentions to her. But why would he take her mother's personal pieces, the items she'd been gifted or had inherited from her own family? They had never belonged to him.

Placing a hand to her stomach, she wondered, not for the first time, if it was a boy or a girl growing inside her.

It wasn't just her mother's jewellery and most of her wardrobe, *everything* passed on by her mother had been kept behind. The same went for her book and art collection, all of the things Catalina had expected to pass on to her own children.

Nothing could have told her more that she was an outcast from her family.

Nathaniel might have dismissed her fears but she knew in her heart that her instincts had been right. Her father and brother had fired a warning shot at her. She was owned entirely by the House of Fernandez. This was their way of telling her that if she didn't behave herself, she would never be allowed back in the fold.

She was doing everything they wanted and still they wanted more for their pound of flesh.

For the first time she questioned whether she *wanted* to return to the fold.

She'd spent her life believing in duty and loyalty. Was it too much to expect some loyalty and compassion in return?

Nathaniel put his files away, turned his laptop and desktop off, checked his phone for messages and decided to call it a night.

As he stepped out of his office, movement behind him made him turn.

Catalina stood half in and half out of the sitting

room, hovering in the doorway. 'I thought I heard a noise,' she said softly.

'I'm just finishing for the night.' He shut the door behind him and kept his hand on the handle, trying not to notice that she was wearing a long white Victorian nightdress with a high neck but also the thinnest of sleeves that showed off her slender arms. Her raven hair was loose and spilled down her back and over her shoulders. She looked innocent. Clean and pure. Yet her innate sexiness shone through.

He cleared his throat. 'Where is Clotilde?' Assigning Catalina a dedicated companion in his household had worked out as well for him as it had for her. He'd made it to three days of living under the same roof without finding himself alone with his wife. Until now.

'She's making me a hot chocolate.' One bare, creamy shoulder lifted. 'She wouldn't let me help.'

'I should think not.' His staff had strict instructions—under no circumstances should the Princess do anything for herself. Frederic had spoken to a senior member of the palace staff who'd informed him the only personal duty the royal family performed for themselves was the brushing of their teeth. The King, however, left even that for one of his minions. It was an alien lifestyle to Nathaniel, even with the vast wealth he'd accumulated, which easily rivalled that of the House of Fernandez. 'How are you settling in? Have you everything you need?'

'Your staff are taking good care of me.' Catalina stepped out from the threshold and stood before him, a shrewdness to her stare. 'Will I be seeing you tomorrow?'

'I'll be at home.'

'That's not what I asked.'

'I know.' He ran a hand through his hair, pretending not to notice that the light she stood under had the effect of making her nightdress almost transparent. 'I'll be here but working again.'

Her lips tightened a touch but she gave the graceful nod he'd been fascinated by for years. It was a nod that could mean anything and nothing. It gave away nothing of her thoughts.

Breathing had become a struggle. The outline of her breasts was clearly visible beneath the fabric.

A seemingly modest, old-fashioned *nightdress* had kick-started his libido better than any overtly sexy lingerie ever could. Because he knew what lay beneath it and the ecstasy he had found in her arms.

She couldn't be aware of how exposed she was; not when she could be seen by any member of his staff. Catalina was no exhibitionist.

He shouldn't be staring. He wasn't a lusty teenager... but, he had to admit, being within three feet of her made him feel like one. She was walking temptation, a danger to him as great as the biggest temptation he had ever known, which had ruined his life all those years ago, making him an outcast from what remained of his family.

His seduction of Catalina had almost made her an outcast from *her* family. It still could.

There had been no quell in his desire for her. None at all. He'd spent the past three days catching up on paperwork but had only accomplished a tenth of what he'd set out to do. The rest of the time he'd spent gazing at the office door wondering what she was doing at that precise moment.

He could tell himself it was concern for a princess yanked from her palace to live amongst commoners that had him constantly thinking about her. But lying to himself was something he hadn't tolerated since he was seventeen, when he'd lied to himself that his libido was stronger than his morals. The truth was he had spent the days thinking of Catalina because her living under the same roof as him had increased the vividness of his memories of their night together. He could see her as clearly with his eyes open as when they were shut.

He might have successfully avoided her by locking himself away in his office but her presence had been with him nonetheless.

And here she was now, her eyes piercing him, her scent tantalising him, her body visibly naked beneath her thin...

'You should think about wearing a robe with that nightdress,' he snapped with an unintended brusqueness.

Her pretty brows drew together. 'Why?' Then she looked down, looked up at the light, looked down again, and turned the colour of a radish.

This was the moment he should retire to his bedroom. He should be far away from her, not fighting the urge to pin her to the passageway wall and strip that nightdress off her.

'I think you must use brighter light bulbs than we use in the palace,' she whispered after moments of painful

silence. Strangely, she made no effort to cover herself or step out from under the light and her eyes held his.

It was only Clotilde appearing from the left, a bone china cup and saucer in hand—someone in his household must have bought them in especially for the Princess because, as far as he was aware, everyone in his household drank from mugs, himself included—that broke the tension between them.

Catalina stepped immediately out of the light bulb's glare and, with only the smallest of catches in her voice, thanked Clotilde.

Clotilde, blissfully unaware that she had walked into anything—*nothing*, he reprimanded himself sharply; she hadn't interrupted *anything*—beamed and turned to Nathaniel. 'Can I get you a hot chocolate too? Or fix you a nightcap?'

'I'll fix my own when I'm ready.' Nodding at them both without making eye contact, he bid them goodnight and disappeared to his bedroom.

Catalina sat in her bed, flicking through one of the magazines that Clotilde had left after sitting in the bedroom while Catalina had had a bath. Starting from tomorrow she was going to start easing Clotilde's attempts to win a Companion of the Year Award and start learning to do things for herself. So far, any attempt at independence other than brushing her own hair had been neatly sidestepped.

While she read, she tried to focus her mind on things she could do to fill her time. As her royal engagements were cancelled until after the baby was born, she would need to find *something* to keep her occupied. The long days stretched ahead of her interminably. She needed to broach the subject with Nathaniel. But not in her nightdress.

Heat flamed her cheeks as she remembered standing before him and the stark realisation the passageway's lighting had caused her nightdress to become see-through. Then heat flamed a more intimate part of her as she remembered the look in his eyes. That had been hunger there. She'd recognised it. She'd seen it the night they'd conceived their child.

It was that hunger that kept her eyes flickering to the door and her senses alert for any approaching footstep.

Would this be the night he came to her? Would he knock on her door, intent on the consummation of their marriage?

Would she let him or would she say no? Royal wives of Monte Cleure were not supposed to deny their husbands. She might have married a commoner but she was still a royal princess. Legally, she was Nathaniel's property and would remain so until their divorce was finalised. Unless her father actively cast her out and stripped her of her HRH title, she remained bound by her palace's constitutional laws...

It occurred to her that the constitutional laws only applied while she was on Monte Cleure...

She heard a noise and stopped breathing, her heart setting off at a canter.

After long seconds of silence she lay back against the headboard and closed her eyes, willing her pulse to slow.

No, she couldn't swear that if he came into her room and climbed into her bed she wouldn't open her arms and welcome him.

And neither could she swear that she wouldn't freeze him out and demand he leave.

She never got the chance to find out what she would do.

Three hours later when midnight was but a distant memory, her tired brain finally switched off and went to sleep.

Her weary but aching heart still hurt when she awoke the next morning.

CHAPTER SIX

CATALINA MADE HER way from her bedroom to the dining room, Clotilde hot on her heels, opening doors for her.

To her surprise, Nathaniel was sitting at the dining table drinking coffee and reading a newspaper, an empty plate to his side.

Usually he only deigned to spend time with her at evening dinner when he would make polite enquiries about her health, exchange idle chat until their plates were clean and then excuse himself. It had been the same for the ten whole days of their marriage.

He stood to greet her. 'Did you sleep well?'

'Yes, thank you.'

She took the seat Clotilde pulled out for her. After a pot of decaffeinated tea was brought to her and her breakfast order taken, she found herself alone with her husband.

'It's a surprise to see you here,' she said. 'You're normally in your office by now.'

'I shall work on the flight.'

This was the first she'd heard of a flight. 'Where are we going?'

'I'm going to Shanghai. There's land for sale that I'm interested in buying.'

'Am I not coming with you?'

'It's a business trip. You'd be bored.'

Knowing a snub when she heard one and too well trained to argue further, Catalina smiled graciously and took a sip of her tea, but inside she seethed. 'How long are you going for?'

'A couple of weeks.'

'That long?'

'Purchasing land there isn't easy, especially for foreigners.'

She couldn't help herself. 'You're leaving me for two weeks?'

'My staff will take care of you.'

'I know they will but that isn't what I meant. Will it not seem strange you leaving your new bride for a business trip?'

Thinking of herself as a bride was a joke in itself.

How was it possible to be a bride when your groom went out of his way to avoid you and ensured zero physical contact? Forget her thoughts that he might come to her; the distance he enforced had only grown.

'Not for anyone who knows me,' he answered with a shrug.

'When do you leave?'

'In an hour.'

He was so blasé that for the first time in her entire life, Catalina wanted to hit someone.

Not even throughout all the verbal and physical abuse she'd had meted out to her by her brother had she wanted to inflict pain back.

Yet here was Nathaniel, speaking courteously to her, and all she wanted to do was rain thumps down all over him.

The fact he addressed her with politeness and courtesy meant nothing when he couldn't wait to travel halfway around the world to get away from her.

'Do you have many travelling plans for the foreseeable future?' she asked, suddenly recalling all the business developments he had scattered around the world.

'After Shanghai I'll be back here for a few weeks then off to Greece. After that I'll be...'

'Can I come with you to Greece?'

He rubbed the nape of his neck and grimaced. 'Catalina, it'll be a business trip, not a holiday.'

'I won't get in your way. I'll amuse myself.'

He shook his head, and as he did so her anger finally pushed to the surface.

'Are you deliberately going out of your way to humiliate me?'

'I have no idea what you're talking about.'

She stared at him with incredulity. 'We're barely married and you're flying around the world without me. What kind of message does that send? And not just to the public but to me too? Am I such dreadful company you can't bear to have me by your side even for a limited amount of time?'

'Not at all...' He blew out air through his teeth.

'Then you have no reasonable excuse not to take me with you to Greece.'

'I don't need a reasonable excuse. The answer is no. I don't need the aggravation of keeping watch over a princess when I'm supposed to be working. Here, in this apartment, I know you're safe and I don't have to worry.'

'I might be a princess but I'm not a child.'

'You are my responsibility.'

'You're making excuses to keep me at arm's length. Have I done something to offend you? Do I have body odour?'

He quelled her with a stare. It occurred to her that he was actually looking at her rather than through her as he had done since the night he'd seen through her nightdress.

Frustration was etched on every line of his face. 'Catalina, this isn't a real marriage.'

'You have made that abundantly clear.' He still hadn't answered her question as to why he was keeping her at arm's length.

'You knew what you were signing up for when you agreed to it.' He got to his feet and pushed in his chair.

'Then tell me what I'm supposed to do. I'm not used to being idle. I'm used to being busy. Am I supposed to spend my time stuck in this apartment watching the clock, the seconds ticking down to the day you can be rid of me?'

From the look he threw at her before leaving the dining room, she gathered that was precisely what she was expected to do.

He didn't even have the courtesy to say goodbye. A week after he'd left for Shanghai, he still hadn't found the good manners to call her.

Unable to sleep, Catalina found herself gazing at

the light drizzle of rain bouncing off her bedroom window. Nathaniel's apartment building was in the heart of Monte Cleure's financial district, a building with over twenty apartments of which she had met no neighbours. Colourful lights illuminated the darkness below, a sign that her people and her country's visitors were enjoying the nightlife Monte Cleure had to offer. It was a nightlife she had never been allowed to experience for herself.

She'd never considered her life restrictive before. Not properly. She had accepted everything. But then, she had never had so much time to *think* before. With nothing to occupy her days, she had so many hours to fill that there was nothing to do *but* think. And one of the things she kept thinking was how much of life she had missed.

Having imagined she would marry one of the Kalliakis Princes, she had always thought that one day she would receive a modicum of freedom. She had hardly dared acknowledge to herself how much she had wanted this.

Then, upon learning that she was carrying Nathaniel's child and that she would be marrying him…a real life had beckoned to her for a few tantalising seconds. But nothing had changed. Everything was still controlled for her.

She was expected to obey. That was what she'd been put on this earth for. No one cared for her personal thoughts and feelings. They didn't matter to anyone.

Nathaniel had at least listened to her unspoken plea for something to do: he'd given Clotilde a credit card and ordered her to take Catalina shopping. He'd given

Clotilde, his *employee*, the credit card, not Catalina. That had hurt almost as much as his dismissal of her attempts to travel with him and the cold shoulder she'd received since they'd exchanged their vows.

She had seen the hunger in his eyes. He did want her. It wasn't that he'd slept with her and become immediately bored with her; it was much worse than that. He had *chosen* to snub her.

He clearly thought her so vacuous that she would be happy to fill her days shopping. She had never been shopping in her life.

Thirsty and still wide awake, her heart aching, she padded quietly from her room, making sure to close the door softly behind her. She was thankful for the thick carpets that muffled her tread. Clotilde had been reading up on a companion's duties and had moved into the bedroom next to hers so 'she could be available to her any time of day or night'. No amount of protests from Catalina could dissuade her from this.

She made her way stealthily to the kitchen, determined not to wake anyone up. All she wanted to do was make herself a cup of tea without having the kettle snatched away with an admonishment that they couldn't risk a princess burning her hand with an errant kettle. But Catalina had watched everything carefully, determined that one day she would do these simple tasks the rest of the world took for granted.

As she passed Nathaniel's home office, the door, slightly ajar, caught her attention. It was normally kept closed.

Curious to see into a room she had intuitively known

was off-limits, she pushed the door open and switched the light on.

Why shouldn't she be in here? she thought defiantly. She was his *wife* even if only in name.

A large oak desk dominated the office, which had a functional, transitory feel to it. Nathaniel, she knew, had properties scattered across the world that he lived in for days, weeks or months at a time. Nothing was permanent in his life, especially not his wife.

If he could be so cold to her, how would he treat their child? What kind of father would he be? An absent one, if his current form was anything to go by.

So who *would* be her child's father? Who would take on the dominant male role? Her father?

Ice ran up her spine as she considered Dominic's involvement. Once she was back in the palace there was no way he would allow himself to be sidelined. Until she was married off again, her father and brother would take control of her child's life.

And she would be married off again. To another man who would dominate her and expect her to do his bidding without argument or question. To a man who would then take control of her child.

She hugged her stomach where the tiny life inside her was at that very moment growing and developing.

That little life was the most precious thing in the world.

A black briefcase on the desk caught Catalina's attention. The room was so impeccably tidy, with everything filed away, not a stray pen or sheet of paper to be seen, that the case stuck out like a beacon to her eyes.

She put a thumb on each clasp and pressed. Expecting it to be locked, she nearly jumped when the clasps sprang apart.

Feeling guilty for being nosy, she nonetheless carefully prised the briefcase open. The very last thing she expected to see in it were the stacks of twenty-euro notes.

Nathaniel and his architect sat in his hotel suite poring over the brief notes James had made on their earlier trip to plot of land Nathaniel was in the process of buying. He'd employed James as architect on his last handful of developments and liked the way he never tried to impose his own vision on the projects. Nathaniel would sketch his thoughts onto paper then sit back and wait for James to produce the blueprints.

The past week had been extremely fruitful. His house-hunting team had found a handful of prospective homes for him to check out too. All in all, everything was proceeding exactly as he had...

His phone buzzed, Alma's name flashing up on the screen.

'Excuse me,' he apologised to James. Accepting the call, he put the phone to his ear.

'Nathaniel?' There was stark panic in his PA's voice.

'What's the matter?'

He heard her swallow. 'She's gone.'

'Who?'

'The Princess. She's gone.'

'How can she be gone?'

'Clotilde went to her room at the usual time and she

wasn't there. The concierge says she appeared from the apartment's elevator at five in the morning and asked him to book a taxi for her.'

'Did he say where she went?'

'No, but we've traced the driver. She went to the airport.'

Somehow he managed to keep his tone tempered. 'Alma, tell me how the Princess was able to bypass the security guards.' He had guards permanently stationed at the three exits of the apartment block.

'The taxi collected her in the underground car park, which she entered using the staff elevator. She had a headscarf on—the guards had no way of knowing it was her.' Alma's voice dropped to a whisper. 'That's not all. Most of the money from your French club has gone too. The Princess must have taken it.'

Nathaniel's first reaction was to laugh. Catalina had stolen his money and scarpered? The idea was beyond ridiculous. Catalina was the most dutiful and conscientious person he had ever met.

But then something snaked up his stomach and clenched around his chest, a sudden coldness freezing his blood in an instant. Had she gone willingly? Or had she been coerced? Was she at that moment someone's hostage?

Had her brother taken her? There was something about their sibling relationship that sent sirens blaring in him. Catalina had warned him that Dominic meant him harm. Did that harm extend to Catalina herself?

'Where did she fly to?' he asked harshly.

'We can't get that information from the authorities at the airport.'

'I'm coming back.' He disconnected the call and immediately called his pilot, ordering his private jet and crew to prepare for departure within the hour.

Fighting to keep the dread at bay, he made a string of calls, throwing clothes in his suitcase as he spoke, not wanting to waste precious seconds by calling staff to pack for him. By the time he was done and hurrying through the hotel's lobby to his driver waiting outside, he'd hit enough brick walls to know he had to call in outside help.

He had to call the King of Monte Cleure and tell him his eldest daughter, pregnant and newly married, had disappeared.

Catalina carried her small bag of groceries back to the cabin house she'd rented in Spain's Benasque Valley, the cold breeze stinging her face. Arctic snow boots kept her feet dry as she safely crunched through the settled snow, her faux-fur-lined gloves keeping her hands warm.

The stone cabin, one of a cluster of similar-looking dwellings, overlooked the frozen Esera River. Her tourist neighbours spent their days skiing, leaving Catalina to the blissful silence.

Inside, the warmth of the log fire greeted her and she shrugged off her thick coat, removed her hat, scarf, gloves and boots, and filled up the kettle.

It had taken her five days to psych herself up to leave the cabin. Necessity had forced her hand when the cupboards had run bare. Now she awoke each morning looking forward to a walk into the town of Benasque. Until the morning she'd walked out of Nathaniel's apartment she had never left a building on her own. She had never gone anywhere on her own before.

When she'd left, she hadn't had a destination in mind, just a stone-cold determination to get out of the country. The compulsion had been so sudden and so *strong* that she'd obeyed; not thinking, acting solely on instinct. She had changed into a pair of ordinary-looking jeans and an ordinary-looking black sweater, covered her hair in a silk scarf, grabbed her passport— only Monte Cleure's ruling monarch was allowed to travel without one—and selected her roomiest handbag. She'd then treaded carefully back to Nathaniel's office and transferred as much of the cash in the briefcase to her handbag that could physically fit.

Escaping the building and getting to the airport had been problem free. On arrival, she'd searched the departing flights and Andorra La Vella had immediately jumped out at her. She'd known even as she'd queued for her ticket that she wouldn't stay there but seeing the name Andorra had brought to mind the town of Benasque, which she knew was over the border on the Spanish side of the Pyrenees Mountains.

She'd paid for her ticket with the stolen money. It had been the first time she'd physically handed money over for anything. The palace had always paid for everything. Other than the raised brow she'd received from the woman serving her when she'd checked Catalina's passport, no one had batted an eyelid at her, although she had heard one child saying to her mother as they passed that she looked like Princess Catalina.

There had been a moment of panic when the enormity of what she was doing finally set in but she'd smothered it with thoughts of her growing baby. Those idle weeks in Nathaniel's apartment had brought her whole life into focus. And it wasn't a life she wanted for her child. If she didn't leave Monte Cleure now she knew she might never have the chance again.

It was the moment she hadn't known she'd been waiting for all her life. It was an opportunity that would never come again. If she couldn't take the freedom beckoning to her for her own sake, she needed to grab it for her baby.

But what had started almost like a great adventure had quickly turned into something far more stressful than she could have anticipated. There had been so many *people* at the airport for a start, who had all been jostling each other, on a mission to be somewhere. Until that point all the interaction she'd had with others outside the palace had been carefully stage-managed and choreographed. She'd given as much of herself to them as she could but there had always been security by her side and an invisible line between them, which the public had instinctively known they could not cross.

Now, that invisible line had gone.

In Andorra, a nice gentleman at the airport had given her directions and assistance, and two hours later she'd been bundled up in cold weather clothes and on a bus heading to the town she remembered her mother talking about from her own childhood. If she'd known it would take almost eight hours to get there and that she would suffer from motion sickness, she might have thought twice and hired a taxi, but she had thought travelling by bus would give her greater anonymity. If not for the sickness she might have enjoyed the novelty of it all.

She didn't expect to hide for ever; indeed she was surprised she'd managed it as long as she had. All she wanted was the peace she'd found to last for as long as it could before she made the call and faced the music. One more day. Then she would tell her father she wasn't coming home.

She put her groceries away and opened the box containing the mobile phone she'd bought earlier. She might have come to a nasty realisation about her family and the twisted dynamics within which it operated, but she didn't want to cause them unnecessary worry. She'd called the palace from Andorra's airport to let them know she was safe and would be in touch soon, then had hung up before Lauren, who'd taken the call, could question her.

She hadn't called Nathaniel. She figured he'd celebrate the news she'd left. She'd freed him of his responsibility towards her. As for the money...

Her face burned to think of what she'd done. She'd stolen his money. She was a thief. She'd never understood how guilt could stop someone from sleeping but now she did, the knowledge of her thievery an unmovable fire in her brain.

But it was more than that. She couldn't get *him* out of her mind.

She couldn't put it off any longer. Her family could wait a bit longer but she would call Nathaniel tonight.

There was a rap on the front door.

She put the phone down on the counter and headed cautiously to the kitchen window to see who was calling. In her ten days here she'd had only one visitor, and that had been the cabin's owner.

Her heart practically flew out of her mouth when she saw the tall figure of Nathaniel standing there.

Before she could hide he turned his head and looked straight at her.

Her heart was pumping so hard its beat echoed in her ears. She never had the chance to get to the door because he pushed it open.

There was a long period of silence.

He glowered at her, larger and more powerful than she remembered, the green of his eyes glittering with menace.

CHAPTER SEVEN

NATHANIEL STAMPED THE snow off his brogues. After ten days of increasingly frantic searching, he had found her.

It was a long time before he could trust himself to speak. 'You have a lot of explaining to do, *Princess*.'

His relief at having found her was replaced with a burst of fury. If she had *any* idea what she'd put him through...

When it had become clear that Catalina really had disappeared...

He'd experienced the most powerful sense of déjà vu, hurtling back twenty-eight years to the day he'd heard that powerful rumble and then minutes later seen the thick wave of snow spreading over the location where the wooden ski bar had been.

The fear had been intense. Overwhelming. There had been moments in his search for her when panic burned like acid in his guts and he'd wondered if he would ever see her again or would ever meet their child.

But he'd found her now.

The cabin was cosy and open-plan, a small dining table dividing the kitchen area from the living area.

Catalina stood, seemingly rooted to the spot, at the kitchen counter, her eyes not leaving his. There was wariness in them and not a small amount of fear, but intermingled with those emotions was clear defiance.

'Don't tell me you thought you could hide for ever?' he said scathingly. She looked surprisingly well apart from the two fingers on her left hand that had plasters across the knuckles. Her porcelain cheeks had a healthy glow to them the like of which he'd never seen on her skin before. She wore black straight-cut stretchy corduroy trousers and a thick knitted navy jumper that fell to her knees. On her feet were fluffy slipper boots that looked, to his eyes, dreadful, but seemed strangely apt for the setting.

These were clearly clothes *his* money had bought because she definitely hadn't taken any of her clothes from his apartment.

'Not for ever, no.' She shook her head from side to side, backing away from him like a cornered cat. 'How did you find me?'

He blew into his hands. The cabin's warmth went some way to defrosting his chilled bones. He'd forgotten how cold winter in the mountains could be.

'By employing my best people to find you. I assume you chose this spot deliberately.' He shook his head, unable to believe the serene Princess he'd desired from afar for years could be so underhand and cruel.

He'd never have believed she was a thief either. Or that she would prove so adept at hiding. By the time he'd landed back in Monte Cleure it had been clear her disappearance was no case of abduction. The call she'd made to the palace had confirmed this. Catalina had run away. She'd taken herself and the little life they'd made together and left him.

To find her here, in the snow-capped peaks of the Pyrenees at the height of the skiing season...

Her chocolate eyes lost their dazed look and snapped into focus, piercing straight through him. He'd forgotten how seductive they could be.

'I'm here because it's a place I've always wanted to visit.'

How could she be so *calm*? Whereas he...he was a ball of lava wrapped in a shell that was eroding by the second, the pressure gearing up to an explosion.

Ten days of worry. She'd stolen a heap of his money but he hadn't been able to stop himself worrying about how she would look after herself without the twenty-four-hour assistance she was used to. He'd expected to find her bedraggled and unkempt.

Yet her hair was shiny, her skin clear and she held herself with the same poise she'd always had.

You could take the woman away from all the trappings of royalty, he thought, but her breeding always shone through. Catalina could be dressed in a pinafore, scrubbing bathrooms, and she would still have a regal bearing.

But that royal body was as womanly and as earthy yet as heavenly as it was possible to get; silk and cream enveloping fire.

He clenched his teeth together. 'A place you wanted to visit which just happened to be on a snow-capped mountain? Have you been skiing?'

'Of course not.'

'You'd better not have.'

'Or what?' There was a flash of fire in her eyes. 'You'll punish me?'

'Don't talk such nonsense.'

'Then don't threaten me. I've spent my life dealing with threats and I won't put up with them any more.' Her voice was clear and steady; only the way her fingers played with the fabric of her long jumper hinted at any distress beneath the cool façade. He recalled her doing the same thing on the drive to his apartment after their wedding, wearing the dress he'd longed to peel from her body, to replace the material with his lips and his body. And then again, at the opera, in that long black figure-hugging dress he'd also longed to peel away.

'I was not making threats, but, as you've so clearly forgotten, you are carrying my child.' His words almost came out as a shout. He was so angry that he was in danger of losing his temper.

'That doesn't mean you have claim to my body or my mind. We're not on Monte Cleure.' Her lips pinched together. 'It wasn't that long ago you thought it amusing that I was happy to let my family have ownership over my body and how I used it. You should be happy that I've taken your words to heart—from now on *I* dictate what I do, not my father, not my brother, not you. I don't know why you're here. I thought you'd be glad to see the back of me.'

He'd thought that too until she'd run away.

'Damn it, Catalina, you're my wife.'

'Really? I thought I was your encumbrance.'

It was the coolness tinged with bitterness that propelled him forward to pin her against the counter.

He inhaled the scent that had played in his memories since their night together and the ache in his chest spread, creeping through every part of him.

Placing a hand to her cheek, he ran his fingers down the warm soft skin, clasping the base of her chin gently with his thumb.

'You are my wife,' he whispered. 'We made vows.'

Her eyes were wide, the chocolate around her pupils swirling, and her voice dropped to match his, her words breathless. 'Vows that didn't mean anything.'

'We made a promise to stay together as a married couple until our child is born. I signed a contract. You have broken your promise.'

She didn't flinch but held his gaze, the swirling in her eyes deepening. 'You broke yours first. You haven't treated me like a wife. If it's a case of living with you for another year and then moving back to the palace while they fix me up with another man who will also treat me like an irritant then I'd rather take my chances on my own.'

'It's not going to happen. You're going to pack your bags and we're going to get out of this hellhole.'

'You can go wherever you like. I'm not going anywhere and that includes the prison you call an apartment.'

'You're coming back with me if I have to carry you kicking and screaming onto the plane.'

Both of their voices had dropped to below a whisper. Nathaniel could smell her warm breath against his lips and lost the fight with his body, surrendering to the quickening in his loins.

Her eyes were suddenly stark. 'Why do you want me to come back? You hate me.'

'I don't hate you.' He hated what she'd done and the worry she'd caused him, but how could he hate someone he wanted so badly?

'Then why have you avoided me at every turn? You treat me like a stranger. I *hate* living with you.'

In all the years he'd known her, this was the first he'd seen of anything approaching vulnerability in her.

'I was trying to protect you.' For all the good it had done him.

'Why?' Her mouth stayed parted after the syllable, so tantalisingly close to his own that if he flicked his tongue out it would press against those beautiful lips.

'I thought I needed to keep my distance because I didn't want to risk you falling in love with me.'

The wide eyes suddenly narrowed, anger pulsing through them. 'Of all the arrogant...' She pushed at his chest.

He stepped away from her and leant against the opposite surface, trying to get air into his choked lungs.

'You have nothing to worry about on that score.' The lips he'd been on the verge of kissing had pressed together.

Nathaniel laughed. How many women had he heard say they didn't believe in love?

'Don't you *dare* laugh at me.' This time it was Catalina who propelled herself forward, moving gracefully to jam a finger to his chest. 'I only slept with you because there was no chance in the world of falling in love with you.'

'Say that again?' Her cutting barbs felt amazingly like a punch to his ego.

She glared at him. 'I felt desire for you. Nothing more. I'd been waiting since I was fifteen to meet someone I wanted and decided not to waste the opportunity.'

He gazed at her, dumbstruck to hear such things from her mouth.

'It isn't nice, is it?' she said. 'To hear the unvarnished truth.'

She had him there; his own double standards were coming back to bite him. He said the first thing that came into his mind. 'Why since you were fifteen?'

'That's how old I was when I found a couple making love in the palace herb garden.'

Taken off guard, he gave a laugh of surprise.

Her eyes narrowed sharply, her finger pushing harder into his chest. 'It wasn't *funny*. It was…' She swallowed and shook her head. 'If they'd been caught by anyone else…'

He would never have expected this turn in the conversation. 'Who were they?'

'It doesn't matter. They didn't see me. I was too scared to stay. But the images wouldn't leave me. Once I knew they were lovers, I would watch how they acted around each other when they didn't think anyone was looking.'

'It was a forbidden affair?'

She nodded. 'Very forbidden. But once I knew I couldn't *un*know.'

Nathaniel could identify with that. It had been impossible for his uncle to 'unknow' what he had witnessed.

'When I found them together that time, I only saw the desire. That's what I couldn't get from my mind. I never knew a man and a woman could be like that with each other. I never saw anything inappropriate between them after that, but the more I watched them, the more I saw they were in love.' Her gaze dropped and she looked down at her finger still pressed against his chest as if surprised to find it there. She snatched it away and stepped back from him. 'It ended badly.'

'Love always does.'

She smiled but it was a mechanical movement of her lips. 'I'm hoping Isabella will prove that theory wrong. She loves Sebastien very much and he loves her too. But I've known since I saw my—' She bit back whatever she was about to say, her eyes losing a touch of focus.

There was the tiniest pause before she continued heavily, 'I only gave you my body. Love is a dangerous occupation for a woman. Especially for a princess. I knew I would have to submit my body to my husband but I knew, whoever I married, that it would be wise to keep my heart and my emotions to myself. The men in my country have all the power. I won't give any man more than what he can legally take.' Her chin lifted. 'And now I won't even give that. I don't want the future that's been mapped out for me any more. I'm not going back to Monte Cleure. And you can't force me to.'

He contemplated her, his mind awhirl, knowing he couldn't allow her to derail him from his reason for being there. 'That's a very pretty speech you've just made and it's very moving but you *are* coming back with me.'

She shook her head with more vigour, her raven tresses swishing with the motion.

'Your father issued a press release five days ago announcing an investigation into Giroud Developments for suspected financial wrongdoings.' Just saying the words made bile clog his throat. It sickened him to know that while he'd been worrying about and searching for Catalina, he'd allowed her father to manipulate the situation to his own advantage. 'He's also confiscated my development and revoked the title deeds to the Ravensberg building.'

She didn't say anything, but her mouth opened and formed a perfect O.

'There has been much speculation in your country about your whereabouts. The palace has issued a number of statements on your behalf, pretending everything's fine, but people are talking. Your father wants you back. You will return with me to Monte Cleure before the rumours gain traction and I will present you at your father's birthday party a week on Saturday, or I will lose my development and my home there, not to mention my professional reputation for life. If I return to Monte Cleure without you, I'll be thrown into prison.'

He had been, in the best of all the English proverbs he had learnt at boarding school, done up like a kipper.

'He can't do that,' Catalina said in total disbelief. And in her disbelief she understood the brief hope she'd felt when he'd held her face—the anger in his eyes a total contrast to the tenderness of his hold—and stated she was his wife. The hope she'd known in those foolish heart-pulsing seconds of thinking she meant something to him…

She'd belittled their night together and what it had meant because she was scared and angry and hurt by his demands. It had been a good reminder of all the things she didn't want.

She'd been right to belittle it.

Nathaniel had come for her because his business and liberty were threatened.

Dominic had to be behind this. It had his fingerprints all over it. Her brother had been waiting for his chance to stick the knife properly into Nathaniel and, by leaving, she had been the one to give Dominic the ammunition needed to make her father twist that knife.

The new independent future she'd been dreaming of was fading fast.

'He's King of his own country.' Nathaniel's tone was mocking but the rage in his eyes was clear. 'He can do whatever he likes but he can't touch me outside his kingdom. I'm a citizen of the French Republic and I have the money and contacts to fight any extradition from a tinpot dictator such as him. But…he can destroy my professional reputation with no effort at all.'

'I'll speak to him. I'll tell him what he's doing is wrong and deplorable.'

'And you think he will listen to *you*? We both know your word means nothing to him any more, if it ever did.'

Of course it never had, not even when she'd been the good, dutiful daughter. Her head spun so fast that motion sickness was in danger of setting in. 'I knew there was danger from Dominic...'

'You think your *brother* is behind it?'

'My father's always been strict and power-hungry but he used to have some scruples. Dominic's influence over him has grown over the years and now he's the first person my father listens to. Maybe the only person.' She flashed her eyes at him. 'Dominic hates you. I *warned* you to be careful of him.'

'I'm not the one who ran away and started this whole ball rolling. That was you.'

For a moment, she thought he was going to reach for her again. It had been the strangest feeling being held by him like that. There had been anger at the root of it but a tenderness in his touch that had made her breath catch in her throat.

Instead of touching her, he folded his arms across his chest—he still wore his black lamb's wool overcoat and navy scarf—and, his face contorted, he continued, 'And it is up to you to put things right. I have done everything that's been asked of me and this is how you repay me? Stealing my money and fleeing the country with my child growing within you?'

'I didn't know it would backfire on you,' she whispered. 'I just wanted freedom for me and our baby.'

'If you had spoken to me about how you were feeling instead of running away like a guilty child I would have been able to help you.'

A spark of fresh fury careered up her spine. 'I tried talking to you but you ignored me. I can see that I should have been more forceful but I have spent twenty-five years keeping my thoughts and opinions to myself and denying my own feelings. It's not been easy for me to change habits of a lifetime and you didn't help by cutting me off at every turn and refusing to be alone with me.'

'Do not twist your actions onto me.'

'I'm not. I should never have taken your money…'

'Forget the money, you took my *child*,' he snarled.

'It was for our child's sake that I left.' She hugged herself. 'My father won't be alive for ever. One day Dominic will take the throne. I don't want our child growing up under his control. *I* don't want to live under his control. I don't want to live under anyone's control any more. You have all the freedom you want, so can't you understand why I would want that for our child too? I was going to call you…'

He laughed and it was the bitterest sound she had ever heard. 'Sure you were.'

'I bought a phone this morning. If you look to your left you'll see it's charging. I was going to call in order to hear for myself what your feelings were for our child and to apologise for taking your money and make arrangements to return some of it to you. I didn't realise how much I'd taken.'

'How could you not know you'd taken two hundred thousand euros?'

'I knew how much but I didn't know its value. I've never handled money before. The palace has always paid for everything. I'd no idea how much anything costs because I've never had to pay or go shopping for it.'

The anger in his expression had gone but a hardness had replaced it. Nathaniel stroked his stubbled jaw and nodded with narrowed eyes. 'You have to come back with me. It's the only way I can save my development. I will not have an accusation of fraud hanging over me.'

If she'd known how to scream, it would have been the time to do it. But Catalina had never screamed in her life. But she had never been so angry and frustrated and scared, not ever.

'I need a drink,' she muttered. 'I'm going to make tea. Would you like one?'

He looked at her as if she'd lost her mind. Which she feared she was in danger of doing. 'Did you hear me?'

'Yes, I heard you.' And now she wanted to shout, something else she had never done before. She'd never raised her voice, never behaved in any way that might be judged unfitting for a princess. 'I thought I'd found my freedom and now you want to snatch it away from me again.'

'I have no choice.'

'You do. You can walk away.' She switched on the half-full kettle.

'Walk away from a two hundred million euro development?'

'Why not? You have hotels and clubs and complexes all over the world. You're a billionaire.' She shook two teabags from a box and put them into a floral teapot.

'Is that why you thought it was all right to help your-self to my cash?'

'No.' She really did feel tremendous guilt for that. 'I know I shouldn't have done it but I was desperate. The opportunity presented itself and I took it.'

'The opportunity presented itself,' he mimicked her. 'Is that what you'll use in your defence when the police question you about it?'

CHAPTER EIGHT

ICE FLOODED CATALINA'S VEINS. 'You would do that? You'd call the police?'

'You'd better believe I would,' he said grimly. 'If you refuse to return with me then you leave me no choice. I don't want to make threats…'

'Then *don't*.'

'There's a permanent video camera set up in my office.'

The ice in her veins solidified.

'It's a security measure I take as I often have large amounts of cash delivered while the banks are closed. The feed quite clearly shows you in your nightwear opening the briefcase, then less than ten minutes later shows you stuffing most of the cash into your handbag. Come back with me and you can destroy the evidence yourself.'

'That's blackmail.'

'It is. I don't want to use it but quite honestly, *mon papillon*, I refuse to let your family destroy everything I've built up. I've never cared about my personal reputation but my professional reputation does mean something. Your father's accusations will hang over me until he publicly retracts them, which he won't do until you return. I will not have my child thinking I'm a criminal.' He flashed her a bitter glance. 'And I want you by my side for the rest of the pregnancy because I don't trust that the minute you're out of my sight you won't take off with our baby again.'

'Does our child mean that much to you?'

'How can you doubt that when I married you to get my legal rights?'

'You married me to protect your development.'

'There were a number of factors but, trust me, the development was bottom of the list. I want our child and I want to be a father.'

As he spoke, Catalina lifted the kettle and poured the boiling water into the pot. The motion pulled back the sleeve of her jumper.

'What have you done to yourself?' he asked, distracted as he caught sight of a surgical bandage around her wrist.

She dropped a tea cosy onto the pot. 'I burnt it on the oven when I was taking a casserole out of it a couple of days ago.'

'And your fingers?'

'I cut them slicing the vegetables for the casserole.' Her body rigid, she took milk from a fridge and poured it into two mugs.

Never in his wildest imagination could Nathaniel have pictured Catalina in such a domestic setting. His chest twisted to think of her hurting herself.

'How do you know how to make a casserole?'

'I can read.' The look she fixed him with was almost, almost a glare. 'I can follow instructions. There are shops in Benasque that sell cookbooks.'

She removed the tea cosy, swirled the pot then poured their tea. She pushed his mug towards him.

'You haven't spent my money stocking up on bone china?'

Without any warning, the tea cosy, which she'd been about to put back on the pot, went flying past his head. 'Is that your entire opinion of me?' she demanded, her voice rising an octave. 'That I'm a useless princess who spends her time worrying about the cup she drinks from? Has it not occurred to you that I have never been given the choice over *anything* I do, and that includes the blasted cups I drink from?'

It was the closest he'd heard her come to raising her voice or swearing.

She took a visibly deep breath. 'I'm in an impossible position here. Whatever threats you make, you can't force me to return. This is Spain. The ownership rights you have over me in Monte Cleure do not apply here. I'm a free woman.'

He almost laughed. 'You consider yourself a free woman when you're funding your "free" lifestyle with money you stole from me?'

'I took your money because I was desperate. I'm your wife. I may not have many rights of my own but even in Monte Cleure maintenance for my well-being and for the well-being of my child is one of them. That's how I justified it.' She caught his eye and sighed. 'But I can see that you are in an impossible position too.'

'So you will come back with me of your own free will?' He'd known even as he'd threatened her that he would never go to the police. But he also knew he couldn't allow her to stay here. She was carrying his child. She was *his*.

The proprietorial direction of his thoughts caught him off-guard.

Catalina had proven herself a woman of unknown quantities, someone who would steal...

But she stole that money because she could see no other way out. She did it to protect your child.

It didn't change what she had done. She could make all the excuses in the world but it didn't change anything.

Nothing could reverse what *he'd* done long ago either. And with Catalina he had tried to atone for those mistakes he'd made all those years ago. He'd done the right thing. He'd tried to protect her from himself and she'd run away.

She's been trained not to speak out, trained like a pedigree puppy to perform on command.

She was speaking out now though.

As all these thoughts fought for attention in his head, she looked him straight in the eye. 'We don't have to divorce.'

He was taken aback.

'The second I set foot back on Monte Cleure, you become my legal owner again,' she continued. 'My male ancestors have fine-tuned our constitution so female members of the House of Fernandez have very little rights, and that means I have no power of divorce. If you refuse to divorce me there is nothing my father can do about it, not unless he wants to rewrite a constitution that grants him so much power. It means I would never have to marry again and no other man would have any involvement in our child's upbringing.'

He listened with his jaw clenched. 'As much as I can see that your idea has merit, I don't want to be married.' He was better on his own. He always had been.

He didn't want to be *saved* as so many women out there seemed to think he needed to be. He didn't need to be saved. He had as much female company as a man could want and he did not want or need more. Not even from the woman he'd married and couldn't shake from his mind. Especially not from her.

He'd thought her different from her brother but she clearly had the same gift for deception Dominic so specialised in.

Catalina had proven herself to be Trouble with a capital *T*.

'I know you don't want to be married; you've probably got a calendar somewhere where you're marking off the days until you're supposed to divorce me. But have you not been listening to me? I don't want to be married either. Not any more. All I want is for our child to have the freedom I've been denied, away from my family's influence, and to live the rest of my life free too. We won't have to live together and you won't have to watch someone else raise your child. Please, Nathaniel. I'd rather be a nun than the property of another man.'

'It could work,' he said with a slow nod.

The more he thought about it, the more he liked the

idea. He didn't want his child raised by another man. His hatred for Monte Cleure had developed to such a degree that he knew he would never conduct any further business there. He couldn't think what had possessed him to develop there in the first place.

The stiffness of her slender frame loosened a touch, just enough to let him see her relief.

'We'll have to return to Monte Cleure and satisfy your father that all is well. You'll have to show your repentance. I want my land back and my reputation restored.'

She nodded her agreement and took a sip of her tea.

'As soon as I have my development back and the title deeds returned to me, I will start the process of selling it all.'

'Really? But it's not even finished yet.'

'The buyer can finish it. I always knew there was something rotten about your country but now I know how deep the poison lies, I don't want anything to do with it. I will talk to the Kalliakis Princes. They like diversity in the projects they invest in and they're not men your father or brother would dare to threaten. It won't be a quick process though,' he warned her. He didn't want her thinking that this could all be resolved in a couple of days.

'As long as I know I'll get my freedom, you can take as long as you need. But would they be interested in buying it?' Her brow creased with doubt. 'I thought they invested in small start-up companies.'

'As a rule they do. Helios was the backer for my first project. Everything grew from that.'

He watched her reaction to the mention of the man she had come so close to marrying. There wasn't even a flicker of emotion in her expression.

'I never knew that.' She considered it for a while longer. 'You're much closer than I realised.'

'Boarding school bonds,' he answered with a shrug.

'How does he feel about us marrying if you're such good friends?'

'Have you not asked him that yourself?'

'No. Why would I?' Her bafflement looked genuine.

'No reason.' He hadn't realised he carried angst that she might still have feelings for Helios.

He shouldn't care if she did.

She tilted her head. 'I never loved him. I never had any feelings for him. But I would have been a good wife.'

Something tight gripped hold of his vocal cords and he had to force them to work. 'I am certain Helios will buy the development, not just because of our old boarding school friendship but because he's been less than impressed at the way your father has treated Amy. But you realise that if we embark on this, it could see you permanently cut off from your family? Right now your father blames me and your pregnancy hormones for your disappearance. If I set you and our child up in another country, he will never forgive you.'

There was only the slightest tremor in her hand as she took another sip of her tea. 'My father cares only about the House of Fernandez and tightening his grip on power. My best interests are never in his heart and my baby's aren't either.'

He gave a decisive nod. 'Then that is what we will do. The sooner we can both be done with your country, the better. Finish your drink and get packing. I want to be gone from this place before it gets dark.'

She drained her cup and placed it in the sink before looking at him again. 'I would like to stay here for one more night...'

'No.'

'We don't have to show ourselves in public for almost a fortnight.'

'We have to put on a united front immediately.'

'What difference will one night make?'

'It's out of the question. Go and pack.'

Her frame rapidly tightened again and her chin lifted, her eyes spitting fire at him. 'When you speak like this you're as bad as my father and brother.'

'I am *nothing* like them.'

'Then don't act like them. For the duration of our marriage—the one where we pretend to be a happy couple—you will treat me with respect and you will treat me as an equal, even when we're back in the misogynistic land of Monte Cleure. Is that clear?'

There was something magnificent about this angry yet concise Catalina. She would make an excellent queen, he decided.

The backbone he'd always sensed she'd had was growing before his eyes. She might be a thief but he couldn't deny his admiration for her breaking free from the box she'd been kept in for so long.

'It was never my intention to treat you with anything but respect,' he said stiffly. Admiration didn't mean forgiveness. And her words didn't mean he could trust her. If she had the same opportunity, would she run again? Would she take his child and leave him a second time?

He would never give her the chance to find out. Until their baby was safely born, he would not let her out of his sight.

'We need to leave now. There's a helicopter waiting to fly us to the airport.'

Her head bowed. 'I'll get my things together.'

Catalina pushed the keys for the cabin through the letterbox of the next cabin along, which was used exclusively by the owner, with a short letter of thanks for his hospitality.

Nathaniel stood by his car, wiping away the fresh load of snow that had been dumped on them since his arrival. From the look on his face, it was a job he found abhorrent.

'Are you ready now?' he asked through gritted teeth. His handsome face conveyed perfectly his true thoughts, namely that she had better be ready.

She had packed quickly enough but had refused to leave the cabin until she'd satisfied herself that everything was as it had been when she'd first been given the keys. She had also gone through the cabin removing the wads of cash she'd stuffed in all manner of places before placing it all into a rucksack she'd bought in the pretty town and handing it to him.

'What if you'd been burgled?' he'd said as he'd taken it from her, his face creased with anger.

'Then I imagine it would have been like Christmas

for them,' she'd answered flippantly, although it had been the one thing that had worried her during her time there. Doing domestic things for the first time had been easy compared to living with the guilt of stealing the money and then the worry of someone else stealing it in turn.

Now his phone buzzed. He answered it and had a brief conversation before disconnecting the call and sighing.

'That was the helicopter pilot. There's a problem with the engine.'

She'd flown in enough helicopters to know this meant it had been grounded. 'Any idea how long it will take to fix?'

'Tomorrow at the earliest.'

'It looks like we'll be staying another night here after all, then.' That was all she wanted. One more night in the place where she had felt so close to her mother.

'I'll drive us to the airport,' he said grimly. 'Get in the car. *Please.*'

Complying, she strapped herself in. Nathaniel got in beside her, made a call to Alma, telling her to notify the car hire company that he would be leaving the car at the airport, and then started the engine.

Dusk was falling as they set off. It was a sight Catalina appreciated as much as she enjoyed the sunsets here.

'If it wasn't to get at me, why did you choose this place to hide in?' he asked after a good ten minutes of silence had passed.

'My mother spoke about coming here when she was a

child. She always said it felt like Christmas.' She looked at him, taking in the concentration on his face. The roads in the mountains were extremely well maintained and the car had snow chains on but she sensed he didn't like driving up here. She attempted some humour. 'I thought that seeing as Christmas was ruined, I would try and capture the magic of it here.'

He answered with a monosyllabic grunt.

'And I didn't think my father would look here for ages. Isabella and I were never allowed to go skiing in case we crashed into a tree and smashed our pretty faces. He thought ruining our looks would ruin our marriage prospects.'

She saw his knuckles tighten their hold on the steering wheel.

'Why do you dislike it here so much?' she asked.

He didn't answer.

'You keep implying that I'm only here because I wanted to hurt you in some way,' she probed.

His laugh was tight and bitter. 'You cannot be so naïve to think I would be happy being forced to come to such a place?'

'I truly don't have the faintest idea what you're talking about.'

'You know my history. I was at school with your brother. Do you expect me to believe he wouldn't have taken joy in reciting to you how I lost my family when he spent our school years pointing out every avalanche tragedy to me? As if dying like that was *entertainment* to him?'

Her brain caught up quickly as coldness seeped into it. 'Is that how your parents died?'

A sharp nod. 'In the French Alps.'

'I didn't know.' She cleared her throat. 'I knew you were an orphan but...' She shook her head, unable to think of the words to express her horror.

How had she not known that? She racked her brains trying to remember if she'd ever heard or read about any hint about it, but Nathaniel kept his private life so close that reports on it were negligible. His school had a code of honour even her brother abided by: never speak of their school years to the press. The press had clearly never found another friend or family member willing to discuss his childhood either.

His past had remained a mystery.

She knew perfectly well why Dominic wouldn't have mentioned it; the last thing he would have wanted was for his sister to have any sympathy for his arch enemy.

'How old were you?'

'Seven.'

More silence enveloped them before he said, 'My parents had taken my sister, Melanie, to a ski bar in the mountains for some lunch while I had a skiing lesson.'

She hadn't known he'd had a sister either. 'Did you...?' She couldn't finished her question; the words lodged in her throat.

'See it?'

She nodded.

'Not while it was happening. But I heard it. They say it sounds like a freight train coming towards you but it doesn't. It sounds like hell. The whole ski bar was flattened. They didn't stand a chance. No one in there did. They all died.'

'Nathaniel…' She could only imagine the horror he must have gone through. Actually, she couldn't even imagine it. She'd lost her mother when she'd been eighteen and that had felt like the end of her world. Nathaniel had lost both of his parents and his sister in horrific circumstances when he'd been only a child. A *child*. 'What happened to you?'

'The authorities called my grandmother as my next of kin but she suffers from chronic arthritis and was in no position to have me. So my uncle and his wife took me in.'

There was something hard in his tone that made her stare at him, wondering what was behind it.

'They didn't treat you well?'

He slowed the car as they approached a particularly tight bend. 'Angelique disliked children. She only agreed to take me on the condition I was sent to boarding school.'

'That's cruel.'

He nodded grimly in agreement. 'I was sent away as soon as I turned eight. My parents weren't wealthy people but they had insurance policies. The funds paid out were spent on my education, which, as you know, doesn't come cheap at that school.'

'Why England though? Why not send you to boarding school in France?'

'My uncle said if I was to be sent away then I should go to the best school available. Angelique didn't care where I went so long as I was out of her hair. I would go to their home every Christmas and for summer holidays but they were the only occasions where she had to put up with me. And even then she employed help to take care of me.'

'Did you live with them after your expulsion?'

He jerked up his chin. 'For a time.'

'A time?'

'A time.'

She wanted to press the subject but could tell by the set of his jaw it would be futile.

She wished she'd known. She *should* have known.

No wonder he was such a lone wolf, always flitting from one woman to the next, one country to the next, always moving. He'd lost his love and stability at seven and what he'd lost had never been replaced.

If she'd known… She couldn't honestly say she wouldn't have taken off as she'd done but she would have called him from the start. She wouldn't have kept him in limbo while she carried his only real family inside her.

'How did they react to you being expelled?' she asked quietly. 'Were they cruel about it?'

'My uncle was never cruel to me. He did the best he could under difficult circumstances. He was in Germany at the time on business. Angelique was there to take me in.'

'Angelique the child hater.'

He paused for long moments, slowing the car again as they approached a small village. 'I was no longer a child then.'

'You were seventeen. In Monte Cleure you don't come of age until you're twenty-one.'

'I thought we'd already established that your country is an archaic antiquity.' Something dark glittered in his expression. 'I was a teenage mass of hormones and rebellion. But I'm guessing you wouldn't understand that.'

'Probably not.' She couldn't take her eyes off him. 'Hormones and rebellion came late to me. Just over two months ago, to be precise, when I committed the only rebellious act of my life.'

He turned his head to meet her gaze for the briefest moment, and in that moment the intensity of his stare was so real and piercing that heat crawled through her, uncurling from her navel and spreading out into her limbs and up her neck.

It was the look he'd given her right before he'd peeled her robe off her shoulders...

The beautiful memories of that rebellious night were as fresh in her mind as they had been when he'd slipped from her room.

If she could take a silver lining from having to return to her home country, it was that Nathaniel was no longer treating her like an opaque ghost. She knew he was furious with her and fully accepted she deserved it, but his anger was a hundred times better than the indifference she'd been living with. He was finally treating her like a real person again, not as the perfect Princess who was judged incapable of lifting a kettle for herself.

The Nathaniel she'd desired from afar for all those years had returned.

The fire that had swirled through her at his stare reignited as she imagined him treating her like a *woman* again...

CHAPTER NINE

THE SNOW WAS coming down thick and fast and Nathaniel had to use all his concentration to navigate roads that were fast becoming treacherous.

All he needed was to get to the airport. His jet was waiting there and the airport staff were used to keeping the runway perfectly gritted and usable.

Catalina must have sensed his need to concentrate for she fell silent again.

If only he weren't so aware of her...

This was why he'd avoided spending time alone with her. Every time it was just the two of them he had to fight with his own fingers not to reach out and touch the creamy skin, to gather the long, thick raven hair in his hands and inhale the sultry scent that had driven his senses wild from the very start. He knew he shouldn't desire someone he no longer trusted, even if a part of him parroted her excuses, trying to justify her actions and pass the blame onto him.

Yet their conversation earlier had changed the whole complexion of their relationship. As much as he loathed what she had done, an understanding had grown between them. For want of a better term, they were now partners in crime, both prepared to put on a face to get what they wanted.

What he couldn't trust was that she wouldn't take her desired freedom if another opportunity presented itself.

'We're going to have to find somewhere to stop for the night,' he muttered as they approached another small town. The snow was now so thick he couldn't clear it quick enough to see through the windscreen before it was covered again.

'I told you we should have stayed in the cabin,' she said, smothering a yawn with the back of her hand.

'You're tired?'

'A little.'

Wiping away the thought of rousing her in more senses than one, he crawled the car through the town's entrance.

Unable to see more than a couple of feet in front of him, he brought the car to a halt. 'Wait here a moment.'

The moment he stepped out of the car, the chill, along with what felt like a foot of snow, enveloped him.

Shielding his eyes with a rapidly freezing hand, he saw he'd parked safely enough. A neon sign with 'Hotel' on it glowed in the distance like some commercialised North Star guiding them.

He opened the car. 'There's a hotel up there. I'm going to see if they've got any rooms available.'

'I'll come with you.'

'There's no point in us both making a wasted journey.'

She rolled her eyes and unbuckled her seat belt. 'Can you get my bag for me, please?'

'Catalina...'

'I don't want to wait in here on my own. They'll have room for us. Have faith.'

Faith was something he'd lost too many years ago to count, on the morning after a snowstorm much like this one.

Of all his memories of his family, that one, of the night before he'd lost them, was the clearest. They'd been in their log cabin, his and Melanie's noses pressed against the window, watching the snow fall in delight and amazement. It had been evening and they should have been in bed but their parents had taken them outside to build a moonlit snowman.

Was the memory so clear because it was his last with them? Or was it just because it had been such a happy moment? If he closed his eyes he could still see his mother's mischievous smile, his father's twinkling eyes and his sister's cute dimples. If he closed his eyes hard enough he could still hear the laughter that had carried through the windless cold air.

This was why he avoided the snow. There was no escaping the memories of all he missed.

He slammed the door shut and treaded carefully to the boot, grabbing Catalina's small case and the rucksack filled with what was left of the stolen money.

Why had he felt like a tyrant taking the cash-crammed rucksack from her? It was his money. Catalina should never have taken it.

He opened the passenger door. She took his hand with her own gloved one and allowed him to help her out.

'You must be freezing,' she said, her teeth chattering. The temperature had dropped substantially since they'd started their drive. 'Take my hat. I've more hair than you.'

'I'll be fine.' He dismissed his offer. His coat was warm. The main thing was that Catalina was bundled up well under her thick snow coat and boots, her hair hidden under a black woolly hat, a thick scarf covering half of her face.

Keeping a firm grip on her hand, Nathaniel led them up the steep deserted road to the hotel, which upon closer inspection was a very pleasant-looking two-storey wooden lodge. They made it there without any mishaps, and opened the front door to a blast of warmth and the blare of distant music.

First impressions were good. The reception was airy and spacious, a place that, while maybe not fit for a princess, was good enough for a woman who no longer wanted to be a princess.

Nathaniel rang the bell on the front desk, which was answered by a frazzled-looking teenage girl.

'Can we have two rooms for the night?' he asked carefully in Spanish. He spoke it well but not as fluently as some of his other languages.

The girl stared at him and held up a hand, then called something over her shoulder in a tongue he didn't recognise.

Catalina pushed forward and said something in what he took to be the same language.

The girl's eyes lit up, and suddenly there were nothing but smiles and sweetness as the two women chattered away. A middle-aged man appeared from a door behind the desk, saw everything was in hand, and closed the door once again.

After a couple of minutes, Catalina turned to Nathaniel looking concerned. 'Do you have your passport? She says she needs it.'

He pulled it out of his inside pocket while Catalina opened her small case and removed hers.

'I didn't know it was a law to show passports in a hotel.' She blinked in amazement.

He bit back a laugh. 'It's a law us mere mortals have been dealing with for a number of years now.'

He handed them over to the girl along with his credit card. She opened Catalina's passport first and was inputting the details on a computer when her eyes suddenly widened and she looked back up at them.

Catalina leaned forward to speak quietly to her, the girl nodding vigorously in agreement to whatever was being said. A few minutes later she presented them with an old-fashioned key and got to her feet, and Catalina took her hands between both of her own. The girl pointed to a door to their left and sat back down.

'We're in room eighteen,' Catalina said, waving goodbye to the awestruck teenager. 'And we've a table booked in the restaurant for thirty minutes.'

He opened the door, which led into a long, wide corridor. 'We have only one room?'

'We were lucky to get that.'

As she replied he caught a trace of her scent.

He could laugh. *Caught a trace of it?* She'd disappeared for ten days and her scent had never left him. It had *fuelled* him.

Gritting his teeth together, Nathaniel said, 'Why didn't she understand me?'

'She only speaks minimal Spanish—this town considers itself Catalan and mostly caters to fellow Catalan tourists. She's only filling in because the blizzard has brought a swarm of guests in.'

'I didn't know you could speak Catalan.'

'My mother was Spanish and was raised speaking Spanish and Catalan. She taught Isabella and I Catalan so we could be free with what we said to each other.'

'Your mother was a member of the Spanish royal family, wasn't she?'

'She was a cousin to the King.'

'Monte Cleure and Spain have strong links, don't they?'

'Yes. They're as strong as our links to France, which is good seeing as we're sandwiched between the pair of them.'

'I can imagine. And I imagine your mother's upbringing meant she adapted easily to life in the Royal Palace of Monte Cleure.'

Catalina grimaced in response and came to a stop by the door with a number eighteen on it.

What secrets would the Queen and her daughters have wanted to share that had necessitated them speaking a language no one else understood?

But it wouldn't even have had to have been secrets. From what he knew of the palace, nothing was private.

He recalled what she'd said about catching a couple making love, and the image of the raven-haired Queen Claudette came to his mind. The way Catalina had spoken, it had sounded as if she'd known the lovers well. Nathaniel had seen the Queen a number of times at school concerts and open days in his younger years, and then at various functions he'd been invited to at the Agon palace, but they had never been introduced.

His money was good enough to be courted in the hope of investment but *he* was only just considered good enough to be introduced to a Monte Cleure princess, never mind the Queen. She'd resembled her younger daughter, Isabella, more than Catalina, but had had the same willowy figure, poise and serenity her elder daughter carried so effortlessly.

No, Queen Claudette was certainly not the kind of woman who would have demeaned herself by making love in a herb garden.

Queen Claudette hadn't been a rampant teenager struggling to contain her hormones.

Not like him, who had once been a hormonal teenager who'd embarked on a tawdry, seedy affair.

'It must have been difficult growing up knowing every wrong move or word would have consequences,' he said quietly, trying to imagine what it must have been like to grow up as a princess in the House of Fernandez.

'It's my life,' she said simply before correcting herself, '*was* my life. I was born into great privilege. My mother never let me forget how privileged it was and I never let myself forget either. And here's our room.'

She stuck the key in the lock and turned it.

The door opened to reveal a surprisingly large room that was as clean and airy as the reception. A carved wooden king-size bed with an enormous fur throw dominated it. The other items of furniture blurred into insignificance.

He turned to face her.

Her eyes were already upon him.

'There is only one bed,' he said, studying her, remembering the way she had trembled when he'd trapped her against the kitchen counter earlier. His body still ached from the remnants of the need that had pulsed through him when he'd run his fingers over her soft cheeks and inhaled the fragrance that could have been designed for his senses alone.

'Do you have a problem with that?' Her gaze was steady and unflinching.

Did he have a problem with that? A problem with sleeping with the most beautiful, sexiest woman in the world who had run away from him, taking their unborn child with her? Yes, he would say he had a problem with that.

At that moment he wanted nothing more than to rip her clothes off, lay her down on the carved bed and plunge deep inside her; to possess her. To make her his.

All the reasons why he'd kept his distance and his hands to himself before no longer applied. Everything had changed. He didn't need to protect her any more.

Hell, she didn't *deserve* his protection any more.

Catalina wanted to make her own choices. If he pulled her into his arms she would respond in the same way she had the first time he'd taken her, with a passion that had caused him to lose control and throw caution to the wind for a few minutes of unprotected pleasure. That he'd kept the sense to withdraw and sheathe himself wasn't a tick against his name. He'd known the dangers and he'd ignored them, something he had never been remotely tempted to do before that moment that had changed their worlds for ever.

If he made love to her again there would be no need to sheathe himself. He would be able to feel every minute of it.

Lust was supposed to be uncomplicated; a mutually satisfying physical exchange. All the loathing swirling in his blood along with his desire for her...

There was nothing to stop him from acting on all the desires he'd harboured for her for years but which had intensified since their night together... And it was that intensity and its potency that warned him to retreat. Because this felt like a damned sight more than mere lust.

'Do *you* have a problem with us sharing a bed together?' he asked in clipped tones, his body tightening painfully as he threw her question back at her.

Her sultry chocolate gaze didn't leave his. Her pupils were wide, calling to him like a visible expression of the scent that drove him so wild. She answered with a slow shake of her head.

Every atom in his body felt charged, straining towards her, fighting his head for control. She was still bundled up in her winter attire, with only the hat removed, but she was sexier than if she'd presented herself to him in a black lace negligee.

He inhaled deeply through his nose, unable to tear his eyes away from the face he wanted to despise but in reality wanted nothing more than to cup in his hands and bring his lips down on hers.

Suddenly her hand reached out to rest against his chest. 'I really am sorry that I stole your money and ran away.' Something other than desire darkened her eyes.

The warmth of her skin penetrated his clothes and sank into his bloodstream.

A contorted smile played on her lips. 'I know you think you can't trust me any more but I promise I will never do that to you again. I'm putting my trust in you and I hope one day you can regain your trust in me.' Now a genuine smile lit up her beautiful face. 'It'll be you and me against the Monte Cleure establishment. We'll be like Bonnie and Clyde.'

'You want to shoot your way to freedom?' he asked, fighting his own smile as much as he was fighting the need to take the hand still pressed against his chest and lay kisses all over her wrist, up her arm...

She pulled a face, her lips twitching. 'Wrong metaphor. Saying that, there's been many a time I've thought about shooting Dominic.'

'Then I guess we do have something in common.' Feeling as if he were disconnecting a part of himself, he took her wrist and moved her hand away, then turned his back on her to open the bathroom door. 'We should get ready for dinner.'

The hotel's restaurant was a large but dark space with tables of assorted sizes crammed in it, all covered by dark maroon tablecloths.

Catalina gazed around in astonishment.

She had never been anywhere like this before. All her dining experiences had been in palaces, stately homes and ambassadorial residences. She'd dined out a few times with Helios but always at somewhere refined and becoming to both their positions; establishments with hallmarked cutlery, chandeliers, serving staff in immaculately pressed uniforms…

This was something from a different planet, from the world of movies. It was wonderful. And also rather terrifying. All these people… The receptionist hadn't been exaggerating about how busy they were.

A young man came over to greet them. She would only have known he worked there by the black pinafore around his waist. When Nathaniel gave their room number, his eyes widened and immediately fell on Catalina's face.

She supposed the young girl at the reception desk hadn't been able to resist telling the other staff that the Princess was staying in their hotel.

At least the weather was too bad for the press to beetle up the mountain and camp outside. From what Nathaniel had said, they would be getting desperate for a picture of the married couple together.

They were led to a corner table, the only free one as far as she could see. There were a few glances in their direction but if anyone recognised her, she didn't notice.

Anonymity had been easy in Benasque. She'd only ventured out bundled up and with dark sunglasses to protect her eyes from the glare of the sun and the curiosity of strangers. Tonight, she'd kept on her jeans from earlier but put on a clean cherry red cashmere sweater, brushing her hair back into a low loose ponytail. Having nothing to change into, Nathaniel still wore his jeans, shirt and thick navy sweater. His earlier stubble had thickened, giving his handsome features an added touch of danger that sent her pulse soaring.

Her blood thrummed; tonight she would share a bed with him. She fought hard to temper the anticipation, remembering the nights in his apartment when she'd lain awake wondering if he would come to her, her heart aching with rejection as night after night the door had remained resolutely closed.

If he were to reject her while she laid beside him...

She didn't know if anything would happen between them but she would not lie to herself and pretend she didn't want it to.

Menus were placed before them and they ordered their drinks.

Catalina read through her menu, then looked at Nathaniel. 'This looks expensive.' The value of money had become something of an obsession to her over the past ten days.

'Order whatever you like.'

'Are you sure?'

He met her eye and lowered his menu. 'Once we've got everything sorted in Monte Cleure, I will buy you and the baby a house and give you an allowance. Until then, I will take care of everything for you so, I insist, choose whatever you like and never feel that you have to ask.'

A lump formed in her throat and she swallowed hard to dislodge it.

'Thank you,' she whispered, before adding in a

brighter tone, 'I've been thinking that after the baby is born, I could get a job.'

His brown eyebrows shot up.

'I was thinking it anyway. I'm not used to being idle,' she said with a shrug. 'And I need to find a way to support our baby when my father cuts me off.'

Nathaniel's eyes narrowed.

'He will.' She braced herself to say it aloud. 'When we finally leave Monte Cleure I'll be cut off for good. It's the only thing he and Dominic will have left to punish me with.'

'I'll support you.' There wasn't any hesitation.

'It's not fair for me to be reliant on you.'

'You've always been reliant on your father.'

'That was different. With my father it was quid pro quo. The palace paid all my expenses and in return I was a princess who brought honour to the House of Fernandez.'

'You'll be the mother of my child. I'll take care of you financially.'

'I do appreciate it, really, but I would like to contribute too. I don't know how to be idle.'

'What would you like to do?'

'I don't know. I don't know what I can do. I'll think of something.'

He nodded slowly, before perusing his menu again. 'You would be good in hospitality.'

His compliment, as off-hand as it had been, brought a flush of pleasure to her cheeks.

Their waiter appeared with their drinks and a notepad.

Nathaniel ordered a fillet steak with fries, salad and

Portobello mushrooms. It sounded so good she ordered it for herself.

When they were alone again, she asked the question that had been going through her mind since their conversation in the car. 'Why did you only live with your uncle for such a short time after your expulsion? You were very young to go out into the world on your own.'

The lines on his face deepened.

'You were seventeen when you left?' she probed.

'Yes.'

'How did you support yourself?'

'With the remainder of my parents' insurance money. It was supposed to pay for another year's schooling but my uncle transferred it to me. I moved to Marseille and rented an apartment. Tiny thing, it was.'

Marseille had been where he'd started his business. The land opposite his rented apartment had been for sale. For years he'd known he would be master of his own destiny and, gazing out at the blank spot on the canvas, he'd suddenly known what he was going to do. He'd called Helios—who was still at school—and told him his idea. A month later the land had belonged to Nathaniel. Two years after that, his first development, a decent-sized hotel and restaurant with a nightclub attached, was complete. He sold it, paid Helios back his money and used the profit to purchase his next plot of land. By his third development he hadn't owed a cent to anyone. He stopped selling his developments after his fifth and had kept all the income for himself.

Thirteen years after that phone call to Helios, Nathaniel had made the official world billionaire list.

'Where did your uncle live?' Catalina asked.

'Paris.'

Her face scrunched up in concentration. He could see her calculating the distance.

'That's the other side of France, isn't it?'

'Yes.'

'Why did you go so far away?' She shook her head in confusion. 'It seems strange to me that you would move so far from your only support network unless you had to.'

'I *did* have to,' he snapped, lifting his beer and drinking half the glass in one swallow.

Then, taking a deep breath, he put the glass back on the table and forced a smile.

She didn't look the slightest bit convinced by it, her eyes piercing his with concern.

'What happened?'

He opened his mouth to tell her that it was none of her concern when instead he found himself saying, 'I had an affair with Angelique.'

CHAPTER TEN

CATALINA WONDERED IF she'd misheard him. 'Your aunt?'

He shook his head, his lips forming into a sneer. '*Not* my aunt. She was my uncle's wife but I never thought of her as my aunt. When my parents died I thought of her as the Wicked Witch of the West.'

It was as if Catalina's tongue had stuck to the roof of her mouth. She simply could not think of a response.

He'd had an affair with his uncle's *wife*?

'You remember the fight Dominic and I had that resulted in my expulsion?'

She managed a nod.

'I told you I was sent to my uncle's home in disgrace and that he was away on business. I expected to be dumped with a nanny or something of the sort but I guess Angelique didn't have the chance to get anything organised. She had to deal with me herself rather than fob me off and pretend I didn't exist.' The distaste in his voice was clear. 'I remember how she looked at me when she opened the door. It was the look the wolf gave Little Red Riding Hood. Physically, I'd changed a lot that year; I'd shot up and filled out. For the first time, she didn't ignore my existence. She plied me with wine, dressed up, cooked me a special meal… I didn't know it then but it was the beginning of her seduction.' He shook his head. 'You don't need to hear the details but suffice to say when she crept into my bed I was in no position to turn her away. She was a beautiful woman at the height of her powers and she knew exactly what she was doing.'

Finally Catalina was able to speak. 'She seduced a seventeen-year-old boy?'

'Yes. She did. She seduced me. And I let her.'

Catalina shuddered, nausea swelling in her stomach. 'That's sick.'

His jaw clenched and he breathed heavily. 'I did warn you.'

She placed a hand on his arm, worried he would think she was speaking about him. 'No, not you. I mean Angelique. What a bitch.'

It was the first time Nathaniel had ever heard a curse fall from Catalina's lips.

'I have to take some of the blame. I let her.'

'You were seventeen.'

'Seventeen-year-olds know right from wrong and I knew very well that what we were doing was not just wrong but, as you rightly said, sick. My uncle took me in from the age of seven. He raised me…'

'He let Angelique send you to boarding school.'

'He did the best he could under the circumstances. He was there for every significant event and that was how I repaid him. The moral compass everyone else has does not apply to me. We slept together intermittently for six months, until the day my uncle came home from work early and caught her sneaking out of my room in only her underwear.'

He drained the rest of his beer and grimaced. 'My uncle threw her out on the spot and gave me a week to move out. He said he would transfer the remainder of my trust fund to me on the condition I moved out of Paris and he never had to see me again.'

'*Have* you seen him since?'

He shook his head. 'I tried making contact a couple of times but he doesn't want to know. He's got a new life now. He divorced Angelique and remarried. He has a couple of kids of his own now. I know he'll never forgive me. He was the last of my family—my grandmother had died by then—and I destroyed our relationship.'

The last of his family...

And she had run away carrying the child that would be the first true blood tie he'd had in a generation.

'Did you ever make the first move on her?'

'*No.*' His answer was so vehement that she believed him. 'I never wanted it to happen. It sickened me but on another level I must have wanted it because I allowed it to happen.'

She nodded slowly. 'When I was at finishing school, I remember one of the English girls talking about her teenage brothers. She said they were *randy little sods*— her words—and that if we ever visited we should make sure to wear chastity belts.'

'Don't make excuses for me.'

'I'm not. What you did was wrong, yes, but you were

practically a child. Angelique was quite clearly a preda-
tor *and* the one in the position of power. She was beautiful and you were a walking hormone stick.'

A walking hormone stick?

Despite the gravity of the subject, Nathaniel couldn't
hold back the small burst of mirth that came to him,
surprised to find he felt a fraction lighter.

He'd never spoken of this to anyone before. His uncle
had never either—the press would have had a field day
if he had. And nor had Angelique.

That his uncle had kept his counsel after the heinous
way Nathaniel had repaid the love he'd given him only
verified the qualities of the man who had taken in his
orphan nephew and done his best to be a father to him.

Catalina gave the glimmer of a smile and said gently,
'The age of consent in Monte Cleure is eighteen. If Angelique had seduced you there, she would have been
guilty of statutory rape. Whatever guilt you're holding
onto, I seriously suggest you try to let it go.'

Looking into the chocolate eyes ringing with such
gentle compassion, he remembered all of the reasons
why he'd kept his distance from her before; the inno-
cence he'd conveniently ignored when he'd been intent
on her seduction and had got them into this situation
in the first place.

He could no longer call their situation a mess. She
was carrying his child. In many ways it was a miracle.

And despite everything she had done, the part of his
heart that wasn't still furious with her knew she was the
complete antithesis of the woman who he had allowed
to seduce him as a teenage boy.

Catalina had been driven to run by desperation. She was only returning to Monte Cleure with him for his sake. Unlike Angelique, she didn't have a selfish bone in her body.

'It's not that easy.'

Her eyes were kind as she shook her head. 'I don't imagine it is.'

Their conversation was mercifully interrupted by their food being brought out to them.

Nathaniel watched Catalina cut into her steak, her eyes widening with appreciation as she chewed her first bite.

Something low in his gut moved, like an intense tug, while a fist clenched simultaneously in his chest.

They ate in silence for a while before she put down her fork to gaze at him. 'What happened between you and Angelique…'

'I can't believe I told you that,' he admitted. He'd thought he would go to his grave without sharing his shame.

He braced himself for her judgement. He'd expected disgust but her initial reaction hadn't been at all what he'd thought it would be. She'd had a few minutes to gather her thoughts however…

'I'm an expert at keeping secrets.'

He could well believe it; after all, she'd lived in the Monte Cleure palace all her life.

'But one thing that has never been a secret is my father's affairs.'

It was true. They had been well documented through the years.

'He didn't suffer from guilt of any kind,' she continued. 'If he was a better man he would have. Dominic's the same as him. To them, women are possessions. You feel remorse. Whatever happened when you were seventeen, you're a hundred times the men they are.'

His heart expanded so much he didn't know if there was enough space in his chest to contain it.

Guilt didn't begin to describe the emotions he'd been living with for these past eighteen years but feeling remorse didn't make him any better than her father. How could it when the cost of his actions was losing the last of his family, the one person since the death of his parents who had been there for him?

He didn't see women as possessions as the King and Dominic did. He liked their company, and not only in a sexual context, but until he'd been forced into this situation with Catalina he'd always known when it was time to move on. He didn't need or want anyone. He was better off on his own. You couldn't hurt anyone when there was only you. And you couldn't be hurt either.

'How did your mother handle the affairs?' he asked, thinking of his uncle's devastation.

She shrugged and picked up her fork again. 'I don't know if his affairs bothered her much. Not on an emotional level. She wasn't in love with him. Theirs was a marriage much as I was supposed to have.'

'A marriage of duty,' Nathaniel supplied, a strange tightness spreading through him as he spoke the words. He satisfied himself that the actions he and Catalina would be taking would free her from the life she'd had mapped out for her.

'Yes.' She focused her attention back on the plate of food before her and speared a tomato.

'Did your mother have affairs too?'

There was the slightest twitch under her eye. 'A woman in my mother's position would never have had an affair. She had too much to lose.'

His eyes asked his next question for him.

'My father has all the power, you must see that. Dominic is second to him. My mother was barely any higher on the scale of influence than I am: nowhere. If she'd been caught having an affair my father could have banished her from the country. He could have cut her off from her children. He could have taken away everything she had—do you really think she would have risked all that for a tawdry, seedy affair?'

He shook his head, instinctively knowing there was more to this than she was letting on.

She put her knife and fork together and pushed her plate to one side.

'My mother didn't have an affair. She fell in love.' She met his eyes. 'It was my mother I caught making love in the palace herb garden all those years ago. It was with the head gardener. I can only assume their mutual love of gardening drew them together. What I do know for certain is that it was no tawdry affair—she would never have risked it if it didn't mean something. They must have loved each other deeply. When she was too ill to leave her rooms any more and see him, I'm sure it contributed to her deterioration. He was so near to her but so far out of her reach. It broke her heart and her death broke his.' Her voice broke. 'He gassed himself two months after she died.'

'Did anyone else know?' he asked, shocked to his core. 'Your father?'

'No one.' She shook her head emphatically. 'Only me. If my father had found out he would have killed them both.' Her eyes filled with a sudden well of tears and her chin wobbled. She took a few deep breaths before looking back at him. 'You can never tell anyone that. No one can know. I will not have her reputation dragged through the mud.'

No one can know. The same words she'd whispered when she'd admitted him into her room all those weeks ago.

'I will tell no one.'

She dabbed her eyes with a napkin and visibly gathered herself before saying, 'So now we know each other's darkest secrets, we both have a weapon to make sure we each keep our ends of our arrangement.'

'And keep our mouths shut,' he finished for her with an understanding nod.

Except the look that passed between them was more than just that of untrusting co-conspirators.

He didn't know what it was or what it meant, but his heart throbbed at it.

'Would you like to use the bathroom first?' Nathaniel asked once they were back in their room.

They'd kept the rest of their conversation at the dinner table light but there had been nothing light about the chemistry seeping its way between them.

He could feel it. He could taste it. And Catalina could too.

She nodded, pulling a washbag and a towel from her case. 'I won't be long.'

'Take as long as you need.'

'I'll leave my things in there for you seeing as you haven't got any of your own.' She met his eye and a light colour crept over her cheekbones, but she didn't drop her gaze.

'The hotel provides toiletries. They're by the shower.'

'Really?'

'All hotels do.'

'Am I supposed to use them?'

Her naivety hit him like a punch in the gut. 'No,' he said softly. 'It's not compulsory. You can use your own toiletries.'

When he heard the lock of the bathroom door, he sank onto the bed and put his head in his hands.

Just when he managed to forget the Princess she really was, she said something that brought it all back home to him.

He could hear the shower running.

She would be standing under it, naked…

He smothered a groan and turned onto his back, his arms arched above his head.

Anticipation filled his thoughts, his body…his veins…everywhere.

Catalina lay on her back beneath the heavy sheets with a hammering heart and a dry mouth, trying not to turn her head to watch the ticking clock beside her bed.

She looked.

Nine minutes and thirty-three seconds. The length of time Nathaniel had been in the bathroom.

She'd left it with nothing but her towel wrapped around herself. He'd been lying on his back. He'd sat up and pierced her with a stare that had turned her brain into mush before strolling past her and into the bathroom.

Ten minutes and fourteen seconds.

The door opened.

If her heart had been hammering before, it thrashed against her ribs now.

His eyes found her.

Only a small low-slung towel covered him, the hard, muscular chest she remembered so clearly revealed to her. The dark hairs scattered in a fine swirl across it glistening under the gleam of the bathroom light.

Not taking his gaze from her, he extended an arm into the bathroom and switched off the light.

Now the only light came from the reflection of the snow still falling outside. The clouds had cleared and the moon was full and bright, seeping through the centre of the heavy curtains.

She didn't need light to see him clearly. He had etched himself onto her retinas over two months ago.

The night she had opened her door for him, she had been naked beneath her robe. Tonight she didn't even have the robe as a barrier.

She sat up slowly, letting the bedsheets drop down to her waist.

His throat moved.

And then *he* moved.

Like a panther, he strode to the bed and, so quickly she couldn't remember how he had got there, she was pinned beneath him and his hands held hers firmly either side of her head.

He stared down at her with eyes that glittered, his breaths ragged and whispering against her lips. His mouth was so close she could tilt her chin and capture his lips with her own.

She wanted him so much there were times she struggled to catch her breath from the ache of it all.

'Kiss me,' she whispered when she could bear the anticipation no more. 'Please. Kiss me.'

The glittering in his eyes darkened, his desire stark. 'Kiss me.'

And then his lips were on hers, his tongue sweeping in her mouth and he was kissing her so hard and with such passion that her bones melted in the wave of heat he unleashed.

His grip on her wrists loosened and she wound her arms around him, threading her fingers through his hair, touching him as she had been dreaming of since their one night together.

Lips and tongues entwined, they explored each other's mouths, his body pressing down on hers, his chest firm against her breasts.

One hand burrowed in her hair, the other stroking its way down the side of her body and then back up again, leaving a trail of fire on her sensitive flesh.

He raised his head so the tips of their noses were touching and took hold of her hand, lacing his fingers through hers. 'You make me feel like I could eat you whole,' he said hoarsely.

Her chest filled with something different but equally acute as the need racing through her veins.

'I want you so much,' she breathed, lifting her head enough to meet his lips again. 'So very much.'

Pinioned beneath his weight, her senses more alive than she had known to be possible, she moaned as he pressed his face into her neck and ran his tongue over her skin.

Slowly he made his way down her body with his mouth. She strained into him, desperate to feel as much of him against her as she could. When he took her breast into his mouth a moan escaped from her throat.

Every part of her felt alive, heat searing through her pores. Every part of her ached for his touch, for his kiss. And every part ached to touch him in return.

On their one night together, his tongue had caressed her there, between her legs, something that had shocked her to the very core. This time...

This time, remembering the pleasure that had re-placed the shock, she writhed beneath him, hoping against hope that he would repeat it.

So many nights she had replayed their lovemaking in her head. So many days too. Always it was there, in the back of her mind. Always *he* was there, in the back of her mind.

His lips continued their caresses down her body, over her navel and down to her abdomen.

Her breaths shortened and she closed her eyes. When he dipped his head even lower and pressed his mouth against her, she sighed and relaxed into his erotic ministrations.

His movements were languid, his tongue pressing against the very core of her pleasure as if he had all the time in the world. Yet as she felt the tension within her grow, *his* breathing deepened. The fingers holding her hips tightened their grip and bit deliciously into her flesh.

The almost painful tension grew until it reached a peak. As her body exploded in a delight of shimmering ripples, she knew this was one intimacy she would *never* share with anyone else.

This was all for him.

Nathaniel felt the change happen. She'd writhed quietly beneath him, hardly making a sound, and then her body lifted as if she was rising off the bed and she released a long, quiet moan.

After a few, silent moments, her head lifted off the pillow and her eyes opened. Catalina gazed at him with a smile of wonder.

Another sigh flew from her mouth and her head flopped back down to the pillow. 'You're amazing,' she said in a breathless whisper.

A gripping sensation caught in his chest, his erratic heart pumping harder than he had ever known.

There was nothing special about desire but his desire for Catalina…it was as if his blood had been injected with a pure dose of longing, a total undiluted concentration he had no control over. He had never wanted to possess someone so much.

Snaking his tongue back up over her creamy skin,

over her softly rounded stomach and in the valley between her breasts, inhaling the glorious scent that drove him so crazy, he captured her mouth for a kiss.

Her hands flew to his head and gripped his hair. Her legs parted, her thighs raised and hooked around his and, without any guidance from either of them, he was inside her in one deep thrust.

She cried out into his mouth and it was the sweetest sound he had ever heard.

He raised himself enough to gaze into her eyes, and they began to move as one, in perfect unity.

A perfect fit. It was as if their bodies had been especially tuned to each other.

A languidness took over him; he was filled with the desire to make this last as long as it could, to exult in every sensation.

Because he had never felt anything like it. The sensation was in every part of him.

He didn't want it to end. He could gaze into her eyes that widened with every slow thrust, listen to her soft moans, kiss her sweet lips and slide deep into her tightness for ever and a day.

He felt her pleasure grow. Her breaths shallowed and became little gasps as she thickened around him. Her head tipped back, exposing her neck, and her grasp on his hair strengthened as the pulsations inside her pulled him so deeply into her that he couldn't hold back any longer. With a cry that seemed to come from his very heart, he flew over the edge, thrusting into her one final time. His senses exploded and engulfed him, taking him far away…but taking her there with him, where they were together as one.

For the longest time they lay there, fused together, the only sound their shortened breaths. He could feel her heart through his chest, thrumming against his own, the most perfect feeling in the world.

Eventually he lifted his head and rested his elbows on either side of her face to stare at her. Then he kissed her one last time before reluctantly moving and gathering her to him.

Wrapped in each other's arms, they drifted off to sleep.

A compression in the bed woke her.

Catalina opened her eyes. Her limbs felt heavy. Wonderfully heavy.

Turning her head, she saw it was eight a.m.

She had woken a number of times throughout the night. As if he were on the same sleeping pattern, Nathaniel had woken too. There had been no words, just an almost drugged sense of their lips coming together and then a fusing of their bodies until they were sated.

Now she looked up and smiled, reaching out a hand to palm his cheek.

He was perched on the bed beside her, a glass of water in hand, his brown hair mussed. She brushed her thumb against the stubble on his jawline, her heart racing at the feel of the heat of his skin. She could smell the muskiness of their lovemaking on him.

Their first night together had been special. Not only had it been her first time with a man but also the first time she had ever done anything remotely out of line with what was expected of her. The fear of getting caught had hung in the room with them.

Last night had been something else entirely. There had been no fear. Just bliss. It wasn't just the intimacy of what he had done with his tongue that she didn't want to share with anyone else. It was all of it.

He was gazing at her, a question in his eyes. She stared back, taking in every line on his rugged, handsome face.

She knew what the query in his eyes meant.

Did he sense her shifting feelings…?

'Is this the moment you remind me we have a plane to catch?' she said, keeping her voice light.

He turned and kissed her palm, his eyes crinkling with the relief she hadn't known she'd been dreading. 'Can you be ready to leave in an hour?'

CHAPTER ELEVEN

NATHANIEL AND CATALINA exited his jet to a balloon of flash bulbs. The newly-weds, who'd kept themselves co-cooned away from the spotlight, had suddenly emerged. The rumours of their marriage already being in trouble had been dispelled by one unofficial press release from the palace and now their exit from a jet.

As the excited crowd, kept back by a strictly en-forced cordon, called out questions and messages of love to their Princess, Nathaniel suddenly understood why her father was so desperate to keep her in the fold.

Catalina was the member of the royal family the pub-lic loved. While her brother screwed his way around the planet under the guise of being on official visits—and many unofficial ones in seedy establishments—and her sister had turned from a wilful brat into a mar-ried woman travelling the world with her new husband, Catalina had been the one who had always been there for her countrymen. She'd visited hospices, opened ju-nior school fetes, publicly supported many varied chari-ties, all while attending functions and charming visiting dignitaries. The people of Monte Cleure loved their kind, beautiful Princess. Without her, the House of Fernandez would lose its crowning jewel.

Nathaniel would bet her father had come to realise this since they'd married, too. Hiding Catalina away as a punishment had only hurt the House of Fernandez. Without Catalina there to deflect all their countrymen's attention, that attention had focused on the remaining family members. Her rumoured disappearance had only made the discontented mutters worse.

'Are you going to miss all this?' he asked when they were safely in the back of his car.

'Miss what? The press?'

'Being a princess. Having the love of your people?'

For a moment her expression clouded then she met his gaze. 'None of it's real. They don't love me, just the image they see. So long as our child is free from palace interference, that's all I care about.'

'We'll be out of Monte Cleure before our baby is born.' The King had sent a message during their flight back demanding a private meeting with Nathaniel.

The hard work was just beginning.

Her return to Monte Cleure wasn't as dramatic as Catalina had feared. The crowd at the airport had lifted her spirits and, rather than the armed guards she'd secretly feared arriving to spirit her away, she'd received a personal invitation from her father for lunch in two days. Nathaniel wasn't invited.

Nathaniel had left the apartment within minutes of dropping her back, citing a meeting that he needed to attend. He arrived back to find her gazing at the invitation.

'I thought this would happen,' he said.

'Why?'

'I didn't say anything earlier because I didn't want to cause you worry, but the meeting I just attended... it was at the palace.'

'And? Has he given the deeds back to you?'

He shook his head. 'He'll give it all back after his birthday party. We've arranged to meet again on the Monday after. He'll hand the deeds back to me and issue a press statement revoking the fraud allegations.'

'That's a start.'

'This invitation is so he can satisfy himself that you're going to toe the line from now on. You need to convince him that you're sorry.'

'I can do that.'

He stared at her thoughtfully.

'What is it?' she asked after a pause.

'I think you should give me your passport for safe-keeping.'

'Why?'

'A gut feeling. Running away was your second rebellious act in a matter of months. He's suspicious. Dominic is too.'

'He was there?'

Nathaniel's jaw clenched as he nodded. Dominic had sat in on that meeting, the look of a bulldog on his ugly face.

The King had been in charge but there was no doubt in his mind Dominic was pulling the strings.

He was certain Catalina's instinct that Dominic was

behind the fraud allegations and the title revocation was correct. Dominic didn't care that the public loved his sister. On the contrary; that was probably what infuriated him so.

'I'd like to keep hold of my passport myself, thank you.' That passport was hers. It was her only guaranteed document that gave her freedom.

'That's fine but you need to convince your father,' he reiterated. 'Show him you're serious about sticking to your part of the bargain. Convince him you're still prepared to remarry an aristocrat of his choosing. Once I get my deeds back I can get moving on the sale.'

She nodded. Convincing her father would be easy. She had spent her whole life putting on a façade for both her family and the world at large. Any underlying guilt at lying to her father she smothered. Her father cared more for the House of Fernandez than he did for her and her child, something she would not allow herself to forget. She couldn't forget it. 'I will do whatever is necessary. But...'

'What's on your mind?'

'Next time you meet my father or have other meetings that concern me, please don't lie about it.'

'I didn't lie.'

'You didn't tell me the truth either. I don't want protecting any more.'

'I'm not used to accounting for my whereabouts.'

'I'm not asking that. I'm only asking you to let me know of anything that affects me. We're a team, remember?'

'Bonnie and Clyde,' he said with a wry grin. 'Okay. I'll remember.'

* * *

The one person genuinely happy about Catalina's return was Clotilde, who'd been on leave on their return to Monte Cleure. She arrived in Catalina's room two days later with a beaming smile that could have powered the country. When she discovered that she wasn't expected to do as much as Catalina's companion as she had before, the smile dropped.

'But I like doing things for you,' she said, her expression woebegone.

'I know you do,' Catalina said gently. 'And I appreciate everything you did and everything you'll do. I still need a companion while I'm here, just…maybe a little less attentiveness, okay?'

'Okay.' Then the smile came back and Clotilde leaned in conspiratorially. 'Julie tells me Nathaniel spent the night in here with you.'

'Did she?' Catalina said innocently, knowing the flush of heat rising to her face would be a giveaway.

Even after their night together in the hotel she hadn't dared to think it could happen again. It had been an emotional day and evening for both of them. They'd both revealed things about themselves and their pasts neither had shared with anyone before. Making love had been a release for them both. A joyous, glorious night of bliss.

On their first night back they'd dined out at a hotel in Monte Cleure. Nathaniel had entertained her with tales of his school days, stories of the strange people and customs he'd encountered due to his various developments across the globe. Neither of them had mentioned her family or their situation. After all the angst she'd been living with recently, it had been a welcome relief to simply enjoy the moment without worrying about the future and what it held.

When they'd returned to the apartment, he'd poured himself a nightcap then, without her knowing who had taken the first step towards the other, she had been in his arms. He'd carried her to her room like the heroine of an old black and white movie, and laid her down on the bed...

He'd joined her last night too.

'She did,' Clotilde assured her. 'Does this mean...?'

'It doesn't mean anything,' she said quickly. 'Would you like to brush my hair?'

She knew how much Clotilde had longed to brush it since she'd first arrived at the apartment, and it proved to be exactly the right thing to distract her.

Soon her hair was brushed to a gleam then expertly tied into a French plait.

'I've been practising,' Clotilde said proudly.

Catalina chose her outfit carefully from her limited wardrobe, now wishing she'd taken up Nathaniel's offer all those weeks ago and gone shopping. When she thought of all the clothes left in the palace, hanging there, untouched and unloved, she wanted to cry at the waste.

Today, she would see if she could have them returned to her. She would have to play it by ear, gauge her father's mood.

She hadn't seen him since the wedding, when he hadn't even bothered to say goodbye.

Eventually selecting a demure black knee-length dress with a collar and long sleeves, she slipped her feet into a pair of low-heeled black shoes and left the apartment.

It felt fitting to meet her father for lunch dressed appropriately for a funeral.

The bodyguards and Nathaniel's driver were waiting for her. The last she'd seen of her husband had been when he'd kissed her goodbye after breakfast. She knew he was meeting with his sharpest legal minds, getting his pieces into place for the coming battle ahead.

Her welcome at the palace brought her much relief. All the courtiers, family members and others alike, were there to greet her. They must have known she'd run away. They must know of the threats made against Nathaniel to bring her back. None of them cared. All that mattered to them was the House of Fernandez and their own positions in it. But their smiles and well wishes were genuine, and that warmed her heart more than she could have thought possible.

It was an even greater relief to find her father's private dining table set only for two.

'Is Dominic not joining us?' she asked after they'd exchanged a tentative embrace.

Her father's welcoming smile was too forced to be trusted.

'Your brother is on a state visit in the UK,' he said reproachfully, as if this were something she should have known.

'Of course.' She smiled easily and waited for her father to take his seat before taking her own.

For the first five years after her mother had died, Catalina and her father had made all the state visits together. She knew he would have preferred to take his favourite, Isabella, with him but she'd been too young, so he'd had to accept Catalina as the best replacement. They'd got on well enough but any hopes of establishing a closeness with her remote father had been dashed. Her father's heart was so closed it only had limited space for love. And that love had been reserved for Isabella. Catalina was able to find comfort in the knowledge that at least she'd had her mother's love. Of that there had never been any doubt.

It had infuriated Dominic to see the sister he loathed having such high status within the family and *enraged* him to see the world fall in love with her. His subtle hints and needling to the King had eventually worked and now he conducted most state visits himself, effectively sliding himself into position to take over the throne.

She doubted her father would abdicate but knew he was proud his son and heir was taking the throne and its attendant duties so seriously.

She also doubted Dominic was happy to be missing this lunch. He would have enjoyed nothing more than to watch her squirm as she was given the anticipated dressing down that was surely to come.

'He'll be back on Friday. I know he's looking forward to seeing you at my party next week.'

She gave another smile. That was all that was ever required of her. A smile of acceptance or approval or whatever particular outward emotion was deemed appropriate for the situation.

Their first course of cream of wild mushroom soup was brought to them. A courtier cut and buttered them a fresh roll each, then put a clean spoon into her father's bowl and sampled a soupçon of it.

When he was satisfied the courtier wasn't about to drop down dead, her father judged it safe to eat.

'That Giroud,' he said between noisy slurps. 'He is mistreating you? Is that why you ran away?'

'It isn't an easy marriage,' she said quietly, casting her head down so he couldn't read the truth in her eyes.

Her answer clearly pleased him, for he chuckled. 'The man is an animal.'

She clenched a handful of the skirt of her dress between her fingers. 'Yes. He is. I'm sorry for running away, Father, but I couldn't see any other way out. I hate living with him.'

'Look at me, Catalina.'

She obeyed and found his brown eyes, so like her own but ringing with malice.

'You have always been a good girl. It's why I decided you should marry Giroud rather than cast you out as your brother wanted—you understand your brother was only thinking of what's best for the House of Fernandez?'

'I understand,' she said meekly, wondering how he would react if she threw her bowl of soup into his face.

'Good.' He smiled. 'You're a valued member of our family but I will not tolerate any further dissent. Lauren will accompany you back to the apartment. You will give her your passport. I will keep it safe for you until your bastard is born and you're married to Johann. He's agreed to the marriage. Your honour will be restored.'

Her heart clattering against her chest so hard it was a struggle to get any words out, she said, 'I don't have my passport. Nathaniel—Giroud—has confiscated it. He doesn't trust me,' she added for good measure.

Nathaniel's instincts had been right. Her father didn't trust her.

The King inhaled deeply then flashed his teeth. 'Bring it to me at my party. If you fail to do so I will have him arrested on the spot.'

He must have seen something in her eyes that she wasn't quick enough to hide because his smile turned into a leer. 'Do not underestimate me, Catalina. I might be transferring much of my power to your brother but I still rule this country and everyone who lives in it.'

Nathaniel knew there was something wrong the moment Catalina got into the car. He'd finished his meeting with his lawyers early enough so he would be there to meet her. He hadn't been thrilled with her going to the palace on her own but they both knew that, for their plan to succeed, they had to carry on as normal. And that meant Catalina obeying her father's commands.

'What happened?' he asked.

She shrugged and looked out of the window. 'He's arranged my next marriage.'

'The Swedish duke?'

'Yes.'

'Don't worry about it. It isn't going to happen.' He

stared hard at her as a thought came to him. 'Unless you've changed your mind?'

'I haven't.' She turned to face him and smiled. It didn't meet her eyes. 'You know that's not the future I want for our child.'

He let out a breath and reached for her hand. He razed a kiss across the knuckles she'd managed to slice. The cuts had healed beautifully, and were now only fading pink lines across the pale skin.

'Is there something else troubling you?' They both knew her wedding to the Swedish duke would never happen.

She gave a brave smile. 'My mother's jewellery. I don't think I'll ever get it back.'

He squeezed her hand lightly, wishing this were something he could fix for her but, short of launching a full-scale assault on the heavily guarded palace, he didn't see how that was feasible.

'How would you like to visit a Club Giroud next week?' he said, wanting to distract her from something he knew caused her much anguish. 'I would take you sooner but I think it's best we stay in Monte Cleure for a while to try and stave off your father's suspicions.'

'Dominic told me they're places full of debauchery.'

He laughed. 'Your brother wouldn't know—he's banned from them.'

'Really?'

'I don't let any old riff-raff in.'

Now Catalina was laughing too; a low, sweet musical sound he'd never heard from her lips before. It filled every part of him as much as her scent always did.

* * *

Alone in the bath, Catalina closed her eyes. She wanted to cry. She wanted to howl. She could do neither.

Her father had her exactly where he wanted her. He knew it and so did she.

Dominic's poison had seeped fully into him.

There had once been some compassion in the man who had raised her. Not much by any means but enough for her to pretend he did love her as a daughter and not just a princess to show off to the world and bring pride to the House of Fernandez. It seemed Catalina's failed betrothal to Helios had killed the last of it and created an opening for Dominic's hatred towards her to pour through in replacement.

As she shampooed her hair, trying to relish the freedom of doing this act alone, all too aware that within a year Marion or one of her other palace companions would be at her side, because a princess couldn't *possibly* wash her own hair, it came to her what she must do.

The freedom she had been so close to having for ever had been snatched from her grasp but that didn't mean her baby's freedom had to be snatched away too.

They took Nathaniel's jet to Marseille. From there it was a short drive to one of the city's most famous hotels. Hotel Giroud. The first project he had undertaken and the catalyst for the fortune he had acquired throughout the subsequent decades.

'I thought you sold this when it was completed?' she said as they entered the plush foyer.

'I bought it back five years ago. It had been allowed to fall into disrepair so I revamped it.'

'It's beautiful.' It was also very decadent. The place screamed money.

The reception staff all leapt to attention when they saw the boss. Waving them away with a grin and words of encouragement at their hard work, he led her to a back office. Adjacent to it was an elevator.

She raised her eyebrows and her silent question was answered with a gleam of teeth. Nathaniel keyed in a code and the elevator opened.

They stepped inside and, moments later, the elevator came to a halt. When they stepped out it took a couple of moments for her eyes to adjust to the dimness. Then she blinked. And blinked again.

'What is this?'

They were standing in a vast, cavernous space with beautiful oak flooring. In the centre of it was a huge round bar, the polished wood gleaming, the brass rail around its rim shining even more so. Dozens and dozens of richly dressed men and women stood around the bar drinking. Dozens more filled the card and roulette tables strategically placed around the room and even more sat at normal tables, socialising and networking.

Music played in the background, a pulsing beat she felt through the soles of her feet.

'This, *mon papillon*, is Club Giroud.'

She twisted round to look at him. 'I didn't know it was part of the hotel.'

'Only those who are members know the clubs' locations, and only those members and the staff who work in them know how to access them. This one has its own elevator from the underground car park.'

Catalina had heard much about these secret members-only clubs Nathaniel owned but, of course, she had never been in one. A club owned by a notorious womaniser had not been considered a suitable establishment for a virgin princess to venture to.

He laughed. 'What were you expecting? Strippers and topless waitresses?'

'Something like that,' she murmured.

'We do provide entertainment at the weekend which is of the adult variety, but nothing that wouldn't be fit for the eyes of a princess.' He leant down to speak into her ear. 'There's a back room I hire out to members. A few of those private parties have been known to become rather wild.'

There was something about the atmosphere of the place, the music and the feel of Nathaniel pressed so close to her that made her quite breathless.

'Come,' he said, taking her hand. 'Let me give you the tour and introduce you to everyone.'

For the next hour they socialised. Catalina knew a few of the members, who all betrayed their shock at seeing her there. After a while it amused her.

'It's like they can't believe they're seeing me out of my natural habitat,' she whispered to Nathaniel.

'There's always been an air of mystique about you,' he murmured back. His hands brushed against her side. 'Would you like to see my office?'

'I'd like to see more than that.' Where the words came from, she didn't know. As the days together passed, the greater her longing for him had become. She *craved* him.

In a few days' time she would hand her passport, her ticket to freedom, to her father.

There had been so many times she'd opened her mouth to tell Nathaniel what her father had demanded of her but she'd always bitten back the words. She didn't know how he would react. They might be having hot, passionate sex at every opportunity but that didn't mean he cared about her on any other level.

She didn't think she could bear to look in his eyes when she learned that she would never be able to leave Monte Cleure, and to find that he simply didn't care. Not for her.

But he cared about their baby, of that she was certain.

Once she'd given her passport over to her father, she would confess and tell him her plan. Nathaniel and their baby would be okay. She couldn't save herself but she could save them.

Now, his eyes gleaming, Nathaniel led her to a door marked 'Private' and locked it behind them.

It was just an ordinary office, much like the one in his apartment, dominated by a large desk and not much else.

He didn't need much else, not when he spent so little time in any one place.

And right then they didn't need anything but each other.

He brushed his lips against her neck and wound a hand round to grasp a buttock. 'We don't have much time. Not unless you want people to wonder what we're up to.'

A pulse throbbed low in her pelvis, so familiar a reaction it was as if her body was training itself to seek pleasure from his very first touch.

His mouth found the lobe of her ear.

She moaned softly then turned her face to find his lips. 'If we only have limited time,' she breathed, 'I suggest we make the most of it.'

'You do?' he murmured, his hand squeezing her sensitised breast lightly before dipping lower to her thigh and bunching the material of her dress between his fingers.

'Oh, yes. I do. In fact, as a princess of Monte Cleure, I demand it.'

His other hand unzipped his trousers and freed his large erection. It brushed against her thigh, sending another pulsation racketing through her. 'What do you demand, Your Highness?'

She raised her bottom to allow him to tug her black lacy underwear down. 'I demand you.'

With little effort on her part, her underwear slid down her legs and fell to the floor.

'Then you shall have me.' Then, without ceremony, he plunged inside her, groaning loudly as he filled her in one motion.

Holding her tightly with his hands on her hips, Nathaniel moved inside her with short, hard thrusts that were carnal and utterly erotic. He didn't kiss her, just stared into her eyes with an intensity that penetrated her as deeply as his thrusts.

Until this moment, they'd always taken their time making love. They'd explored every inch of each other and the few inhibitions she'd ever had around him had been shorn away in their time together. Every coupling had stripped her back a little more and now she was putty in his hands.

He was everything she wanted and everything she needed. She knew now she'd been in love with him for years and couldn't imagine her life without him.

But she would *have* to imagine it because that day would come. Until then...

Grabbing his buttocks to drive him deeper inside her, she felt the pulsations in her grow quickly. He knew the exact amount of pressure and the precise amount of friction needed to bring her to a peak. He knew her body as well as she did.

She buried her face in the curve of his neck as she came, her cries of pleasure muffled by the warmth of his musky skin. With the tremors still rippling through her, Nathaniel threw back his head and shuddered, his fingers biting into her flesh until the pulsing abated. He wrapped his arms around her and held her tightly to him.

She could feel the strength of his heartbeat, the touch of his fingers through the fabric of her dress as he made little swirls on her back.

She pressed her palms to his cheeks and brought her lips to his, then pulled away a little to look at him.

Despite her best laid plans, she really had fallen in love with him.

She'd learned from her mother that loving someone wasn't a choice but Catalina had been arrogant enough to think she was different, that she could make herself immune to the emotion and prevent it from happening by sheer willpower alone.

Was *this* what her mother had felt for her lover? Had she fought the attraction? She must have done. She'd known the dangers better than anyone. She'd known it could never be.

But love didn't care for danger or willpower. It crept up on you so subtly that it was burrowed into your skin before you knew it was there.

Once lodged in the heart, love was impossible to remove.

And now that it was there she would care for it with everything she had. If, to protect Nathaniel and their baby, she had to submit her life to the will of her father and brother for ever, then that was what she would do.

CHAPTER TWELVE

THE KING'S BIRTHDAY celebrations were something the whole country always looked forward to, and this year's party was no exception. Catalina doubted anyone was more excited than Clotilde, and she wasn't even invited.

For Clotilde, the excitement lay in dressing Catalina up as a princess and she was crestfallen when she was told Aliana would be joining them shortly, by order of the King, to help.

'I normally have three companions,' Catalina said to her, biting down her amusement. 'It takes all three of them to get me ready for these occasions, so you'll have just as much work to do to make me look beautiful.'

'You're always beautiful.' A sly but hopeful expression crossed the young woman's face. 'Can I brush your hair?'

Grinning, Catalina handed the hairbrush to her and took a seat at her dressing table.

When Aliana arrived, the two companions sized each other up, both looking to establish their dominance. Catalina was prepared for this and had already written a list of their individual duties.

'Why does she get to do your manicure and I have to do your pedicure?' Clotilde demanded in a sulky tone.

'At the next big palace event, you can swap lists.'

The pair of them bickered throughout the afternoon. It was a welcome distraction. Nerves were growing in her gut. The nausea she'd thought gone for good was back.

Aliana had just placed one last pin in Catalina's hair and pulled the last curled tendril down when there was a knock on her door.

'That will be Nathaniel,' Clotilde squealed, as she ran to open it. 'I can't wait to see his face!'

His face was, indeed, something to behold. He took one look at her and his green eyes widened.

'You look beautiful,' he said simply.

She wore a floor-length petrol-blue gown with a high neck and thin sequined straps for sleeves. On her feet were silver heels that glittered when the light caught them. It was still too early for her to be obviously pregnant but her body had changed considerably. Her breasts were fuller, her waist thicker; all the signs were there for everyone to see if they paid attention. And she had no doubt there would be attention focused on her tonight. Lots of it.

The only attention she wanted was from Nathaniel, who was looking more handsome than she had ever seen him, wearing a black dinner jacket that made her think vaguely of dangerous spies and hard liquor.

In the weeks since their return from Benasque, they hadn't spent a night apart.

He stepped into the room and handed her a long, thin box.

Hands trembling slightly, Catalina opened it to find a gold choker with a diamond-shaped sapphire hanging in the centre.

'This is for me?' she whispered.

'Do you like it?'

'I love it.'

Clotilde was practically bouncing. 'He made me describe your dress so he could choose something to match.'

Three days ago, Catalina had gone on her first shopping trip, specifically to buy a ball gown. Nathaniel had given her the credit card. When she'd tried to return it, he'd told her to keep it.

Now his lips curved. 'Shall I put it on for you?'

'Please.'

She turned her back to him and blinked hard, trying to hold back the tears welling at such an unexpected, thoughtful gift.

When he was done, he placed a kiss to the top of her spine and twisted her around. 'Are you ready?'

She nodded and fixed the old serene mask in place. She was as ready as she could hope to be.

The palace shone against the dark Monte Cleure skies. Lines of cars queued up, ferrying their eager guests to the venue. Nathaniel looked out of his window and wondered where the dread resting in his stomach had come from.

He didn't expect tonight to be easy. It couldn't be. Everyone would be watching them together, speculating.

Catalina sat silently beside him, clutching her silver bag as if afraid to let it go.

She looked truly dazzling. His true Princess.

But there was something in her manner that made him think her façade was hiding more than usual. He'd felt it since her lunch with her father, and not for the first time he wished she hadn't been so well trained not to show what she was thinking. She was too good at keeping things close.

He'd hoped she would confide in him and tried to convince himself it really was nothing more than her being upset at the denial of her mother's jewellery.

He no longer worried that she would flee with their child again. He couldn't say why he felt such certainty but he did. He was beginning to trust her.

Eventually they snaked their way to the palace courtyard. Courtiers were there to assist them out of the car. When they saw the royal Princess had arrived, their attentiveness tripled and they were whisked inside and on to the reception room without further ado.

The King and his heir were there to greet their guests with a champagne reception. When they saw Catalina and Nathaniel, they came over to them, welcoming smiles on their faces, ice in their eyes.

Everyone in the room was watching them.

'Happy birthday, Father,' Catalina said, curtseying to him. She nodded imperceptibly at her handbag, indicating the location of her passport.

The King took his daughter in his arms and kissed both of her cheeks, then extended his hand to Nathaniel, who shook it.

Dominic then offered his hand too along with a grin that looked like something a lion would give before it devoured its prey. Nathaniel contented himself with squeezing the Prince's hand hard enough to break bone then had to watch while Dominic kissed Catalina on both cheeks.

She returned the greeting, taking his hand as she did so and whispering something in his ear that made Dominic smile.

Only Nathaniel saw the slight wrinkling of her nose. They were both too well practised in public displays of sibling affection to do anything but perform. And, he had to admit, they both performed admirably. They looked as close as two siblings could be.

No one there to witness this greeting could think that this was anything other than a happy family.

Catalina's spirits sank with every passing minute and she fought hard to keep the smile on her face. She was out of practice; that was all.

Seeing all the champagne flutes being passed around made her wish she could have a glass or five herself. It would make getting through the evening, her first public appearance since her wedding, more bearable.

As the reception filled up and more guests made their way over for an introduction, the harder she found it to hold onto her mask. She was used to scrutiny but tonight it felt magnified, as if a lens had been placed on her and everyone were peering through it, dissecting her body.

'I need to borrow your husband for a minute,' her father said, as the guests started making their way to the ballroom.

She met Nathaniel's eyes.

His gaze was steady. *I'll be fine,* the look he gave her seemed to say.

And he would be. She would make sure of it. She *was* making sure of it.

Her heart thumping, she watched them depart together, Dominic trailing in their wake.

Just as she thought the evening couldn't get any worse, the second she entered the ballroom, Marion appeared at her side.

'You look fabulous,' her cousin and former companion cried. 'I can see you're already eating for two.'

What she wouldn't give to slap that supercilious smile off Marion's face.

'There is so much to tell you,' Marion continued, oblivious to Catalina's private feelings, and proceeded to impart all the gossip she had missed out on in her time away from the palace.

It was nothing but insubstantial idle chatter but listening to it and hearing the venom and glee behind each sorry tale was like having barbs cast into her skin. People were still coming over to her, interrupting Marion's monologues to say hello to the Princess and see for themselves if there was any truth to the hundreds of rumours that were circulating.

Her lungs seemed to be shrinking, the air around her thickening.

'I need some air,' she said to Marion, unable to hear one more poisonous word or take another sweaty handshake or an assault of someone else's scent.

She didn't give her cousin time to respond, but

promptly turned on her heel, escaping back through the reception room and through to a wide corridor.

Passing a few courtiers with a smile, she stepped out onto the terrace that overlooked the palace's private beach and breathed in the salty air, lifting her face to the wintry breeze that cooled her skin.

Any peace she hoped to find was snatched away when heavy footsteps closed in on her.

'If it isn't pretty Catalina.'

'Go away, Dominic.' She wasn't in the mood for her brother's version of niceties.

'That's not a nice way to talk to your brother.' He leant against the stone balustrade beside her.

She gave a slight shake of her head, wishing she could swat him away like a pesky fly.

'Do not ignore me,' Dominic said with menace in his voice. 'Have you brought your passport with you?'

'Yes.'

'Hand it over.'

'I'll give it to Father.'

'I'm telling you to give it to me.'

She took a breath and faced him. 'I'll give it to Father later. You don't own me, Dominic. Not any more. I belong to Nathaniel and I don't have to take orders from you.' Whatever happened in the future she would never allow her brother to bully her again.

His hand whipped out to grab her wrist before she knew what was happening. 'You're always so calm and collected,' he derided. 'The perfect little Princess; the people's favourite. But I always knew the truth about you.'

'Let go of me,' she snapped.

His grip tightened. 'You are in no position to tell me to do anything.'

'If you don't let go of my wrist I will scream.'

His eyes narrowed. He wasn't used to her talking back. If she screamed then people would come running. They would see.

'Get your hands off my wife.'

Dominic froze.

Standing two feet away from them, towering over them menacingly, stood Nathaniel.

Dominic's hold on her wrist dropped and he straightened.

Nathaniel closed the gap between them. 'If you ever lay a finger on my wife again, I will...'

'What?' Dominic said with a sneer. 'You'll hit me over this worthless slut?'

Something dark flashed across Nathaniel's face. Then his elbow drew back before his arm shot forward like a bullet, his fist connecting with Dominic's abdomen with such force the Prince doubled over on the spot and fell to the floor with a thud.

Nathaniel crouched over him. 'Next time it will be your face.'

He stood, took hold of Catalina's hand, and led her away from her groaning brother. 'We need to leave.'

'We can't.'

'Lina, we need to go now. We haven't got much time.'

She shook her hand from his and stopped. Looking back over her shoulder, she could see her brother rising.

'You shouldn't have done that,' she whimpered, suddenly terrified. 'There will be consequences.'

'Which is why we need to leave now.' He took her hand again and tugged. 'Come *on*.'

'There's something I need to do first,' she said, panic setting in.

'If it's to do with handing your passport to your father then you can forget about it.'

'You know?'

He nodded grimly. They were now at the wide palace door, which was still open to allow late arrivals to slip through. 'Dominic mentioned it to me when your father bore me off. He couldn't resist telling me they had you back under control. You've got the passport here.' It wasn't a question.

'He'll have you arrested.' She stopped at the top of the concrete steps. 'Don't you understand that? He doesn't trust me at all. If I don't give him my passport he'll have you locked up for the rest of your life.'

'He'll have to find me first.'

Still holding her hand tightly but without the malice of her brother's hold, he led her down the steps. Once in the courtyard, Catalina had to run to keep pace with him.

A long sleek car flashed its lights at them.

Only when they were settled in the back and his driver had put his foot down did Nathaniel allow himself to breathe.

No sooner had his lungs started working than Catalina rounded on him.

'What did you think you were doing hitting him?'

she demanded, her voice shrill. 'Dominic could have you killed.'

It took him a few good lungfuls of air before he found his voice. 'I don't care what he does to me. How long has he been abusing you?'

The way her body stiffened told him the gut feeling he'd had these past few months had been correct.

'Catalina?' he said, when she seemed to shrink into herself. 'I asked you a question. Seeing as I've just added a charge of treason to my other so-called crimes in this country, the least you can do is tell me the truth.'

'It's hard for me to talk about it,' she said, her words barely more than a whisper. 'It feels disloyal.'

'Forget loyalty. Your family don't know the meaning of it.'

Another long silence stretched out but then she gave a sharp nod. 'Dominic... Yes. He does on occasion strike me. But rarely anything that will leave a mark,' she added, as if that excused it.

'Does your father know?'

'I don't know. Dominic has loathed me since I was born and father rarely did anything to stop his cruelty when we were children.' A sad smile lifted the corners of her mouth. 'Dominic resented me being born and taking our mother's attention away from him. Don't get me wrong, Dominic's never beaten me. I suppose I've always taken it because I accepted it as his right. Women of the House of Fernandez are supposed to be submissive to the will of their men. But it isn't his right. When I return to the palace, I will put a stop to it.'

'How?' He delivered the word like a bullet.

'I will scream. I will scratch his eyes out. He's not used to me answering or fighting back.'

'You will do none of those things because you are never setting foot in that palace again.'

He had suspected something like this but having his suspicions confirmed still hit him like a punch to the gut.

The House of Fernandez was more poisonous than he could ever have dreamt.

Was it any wonder she'd grabbed her first chance at freedom and run away? She'd been a prisoner in the palace, constantly on edge about putting a foot out of line, paraded in front of the public, who loved her like a performing puppy, then forced into marriage with a man—him—who'd treated her with indifference. The future looming ahead would have seen her returned to the palace and forced into a second indifferent marriage... She should have run further. She should have run to the ends of the earth to escape that fate.

And here she was, preparing to accept that very fate in order to save him.

'I have to,' she said. 'Or you will lose everything.'

'I thought you didn't want our baby raised here. How can you...?'

She shook her head so violently that tendrils of hair fell from where they had been so elegantly pinned. '*You're* going to raise our child.'

'*What?*'

'I've thought it all out.' She spoke quickly, urgently. 'My father still expected us to stay together until the baby was born. He would have had my passport but that was because he didn't trust me not to run away again. That wouldn't stop *you* leaving the country. I would have had our baby here and then I was going to get you to take him or her as far away from Monte Cleure as you could get.'

Such disbelief ran through him that he couldn't get a thought or a word to form.

'And now you've ruined everything.' With that, she burst into tears. '*Why* did you hit him? He wouldn't have hurt me, not with all those guests around.'

'You were going to give me our child?' That was all he could think. She had been planning to hand their child over to him.

Her cheeks sodden with tears, she nodded. 'It was the only way to be sure you would both be safe.'

In the distance came the sound of sirens. He didn't know if they meant they were being pursued but it was enough to snap him into action. He pressed the button to drop the partition dividing them from his driver.

'Take us to the heliport,' he snapped. 'Quickly.' Then he called the company he always chartered helicopters from and offered a quarter of a million euros if they could get a pilot there to take them into France within the next ten minutes.

Fortune was on his side. A pilot had landed only fifteen minutes before and hadn't yet left for home.

Then he called Alma and told her to get the staff together to gather his and Catalina's personal belongings, get onto his jet, and meet him in Marseille. Right now. No questions.

When Dominic had so gleefully mentioned Catalina's passport, her strange mood had suddenly made sense. He'd known in that moment he had to get her out of the country.

Once his private audience with the King, who'd wanted only to put on an act of establishing dominance, was complete, he'd called his driver and told him to prepare to take them into France.

Now there was no chance of reaching the border; not now he'd punched the heir to the throne in his own palace.

For months Nathaniel had wondered about Catalina's relationship with her brother, but seeing the evidence right there before his eyes, the way Dominic's fleshy fingers had bitten into her smooth flesh, the evil radiating from his eyes...

He'd snapped.

The pilot was ready for them and they were in the air as soon as they were safely strapped in.

When they were a couple of hundred feet in the air, Nathaniel looked out of the window to see half a dozen sirens flashing, making their way to the heliport.

He didn't release another full breath until they were in French airspace.

During all of this, Catalina hadn't uttered a word. She sat rigid, her usual poise gone, tears streaming silently down her face.

'We're safe,' he said softly.

She blinked and rubbed her eyes. 'We're never going to be safe.'

'Your father's power only exists within Monte Cleure.'

She looked away again, her fingers playing with the fabric of the skirt of her dress.

Nathaniel closed his eyes and rubbed his temples. Unsurprisingly, he had a headache forming.

'Where do you want to go?' he asked after another ten minutes had passed.

She stared at him blankly.

'Name a country. Any country. Of all the places in the world you've wanted to go to or have been to and really enjoyed. Name one.'

'America,' she whispered after a long pause. 'New York. I've always wanted to go there.'

'New York with a loft apartment?'

She nodded, another tear streaking down her face.

'Then New York it shall be.'

Alma had arranged for a car to meet them in Marseille. In silence they drove to the airport.

Catalina stared out at streets and roads she had travelled past only a few days before, wondering how she came to be here again.

Had all that really happened?

Had Nathaniel really punched Dominic?

Terror took great big bites out of her stomach, acid burning through her throat.

What had he done? Nathaniel would never be able to set foot on Monte Cleure again. Everything they'd been fighting for him to keep…he'd lost it.

And it was all her fault.

CHAPTER THIRTEEN

THE HOUSEHOLD STAFF were at the airport waiting for them in a private room. They were all white-faced.

As soon as they walked in, Nathaniel went straight to Clotilde. 'You're to fly with Catalina to New York.'

Clotilde nodded solemnly.

He addressed the others. 'We'll stay in my hotel here for the night then when the jet returns we'll fly to...'

He felt a sharp tug on the sleeve of his dinner jacket. Catalina, paler than anyone, her eyes red-rimmed, said, 'Aren't you coming with me?'

His nostrils flared as he looked at her. He shook his head. 'I'm going to Agon.'

'I can go with you.'

'No. This is where we part company. If you're not happy in New York we will find somewhere else for you to live.'

'Part company? What do you mean?'

He closed his eyes before fixing them back on her. 'This is where we put our plan into action. Everything we talked about. This, *mon papillon*, is where you get your freedom. I know it's rather more dramatic than we'd anticipated but things have developed in a way neither of us could have predicted.'

'But what about you? My father hasn't given you back the deeds yet. He hasn't revoked that statement of fraud against you.'

He shrugged. None of that mattered any more. 'I haven't a hope in hell of getting anything back now, and I don't care. Your safety and that of our baby are all that matter. Do you have the credit card I gave you?'

She nodded blankly.

'It's got unlimited credit on it. Buy whatever you need—I mean it, Lina, whatever you need.'

'You can come with me,' she whispered. 'We can be a family.'

His heart banged ferociously beneath his ribs as a sudden vision of him, Catalina and their baby together forced its way into his mind.

It was an image he'd refused to see before, too fantastical for him to allow it.

And then he looked back to her sweet, tear-stained face and felt a pain in his chest so deep and dark that it ripped right into his core.

He'd loved his family with all his pure, innocent heart and then he'd lost them.

He'd loved his uncle, who had done his best to treat him like a son, but had betrayed his love in the most heinous way and lost him too.

Everyone he'd ever loved he'd lost.

He breathed deeply and shook his head, denying the words that fought on his tongue, denying the clamouring of his heart trying to jump from his chest and into hers.

He didn't deserve her. He would rather die than hurt her.

'I will be in touch in a few days. Clotilde can reach me if need be.'

It took an age for it to penetrate Catalina's brain that this meant goodbye. That this was where they went their separate ways. That in future she would only speak to him to discuss things to do with their baby, that she would only see him for baby visitations or handovers. That the wishes she'd kept so deep within herself and never allowed herself to dream of, not even in her private imaginings, had at last been vocalised and rejected.

By the time the facts had really had sunk in, Nathaniel had left the private room. Only Clotilde remained with her. The others had gone with him, whispering goodbyes she had been too shell-shocked to acknowledge.

'Where's he gone?' she asked, whipping her head round to face Clotilde, who could only shake her head.

'I don't know,' she mouthed.

Catalina pushed the door open and gazed around.

The airport was busy but not heaving. She could see individuals clearly. But she couldn't see *him*.

Her lungs opened up before her brain knew what they were doing, her vocal cords opening with them to scream his name. *'Nathaniel!'*

People stopped to stare at her. He wasn't one of them.

She began to run, screaming his name over and over, pushing past people, sending luggage flying until a pair of arms took hold of her and wrapped around her waist, and she cried harder than ever to find that it wasn't him but Clotilde, who was sobbing too as she tried so hard to restrain her.

Catalina's bodyguards—she hadn't even known they were there—materialised and, with a kindness that belied their size and power, took the distraught women into their arms and guided them back to the private room to await their flight.

New York was okay. Now she was finding her feet, Catalina quite liked it there.

When they'd landed, a fresh security crew had been there to meet them. They'd been whisked straight to a loft conversion in lower Manhattan with the tightest of security. Catalina had been told that if she didn't like it, there were a dozen other lofts for her to look at.

She'd been so tired she hadn't been able to think straight and had decided to bed down there for the night. The late winter sun had awoken her the next day and, although she was jet-lagged and heartsick, she'd felt a kind of peace steal over her. She'd decided to stay.

That had been a month ago.

Everywhere she went, security followed but they managed to be unobtrusive. There were times she would walk around Times Square or Central Park and forget they were there.

Her 'abduction' had been headline news. So crazy had the rumours been—fuelled of course by the palace—that she'd called and left a message for her father, telling him in no uncertain terms that if he didn't stop the stories and drop the allegations against Nathaniel, she would sell her story to the press and bare all the House of Fernandez's dirty laundry with it. For good measure, she'd then walked into one of the major New York newspaper offices and issued a statement. It had been filmed for authenticity. In it she had insisted she'd left Monte Cleure of her own free will and vehemently denied that her husband was capable of any kind of fraud. He was, she'd insisted, a good man. To the rumours that they'd gone their separate ways, she would only say that she wished him nothing but the best.

What she'd left unsaid was that there was a hole in her heart that she didn't know how to begin repairing.

Returning to her loft after a wander around the National Museum, where even the magnificent artefacts had failed to hold her interest for longer than a few minutes at a time, she called out to Clotilde but received no reply.

That was strange. Clotilde had snapped back into her usually cheerful mood on their first full day in New York. The younger woman had been a godsend and Catalina would be grateful for ever that Nathaniel had insisted she travel with her.

Oh, but she didn't want to think about him. Thinking about him made the hole in her heart rip a little bit wider. Some days she would look out of her bedroom window just as her mother had done when she'd been too ill to leave her room. Her mother had stood there looking for Juan, desperate to catch a glimpse of him. And Juan would often sit under the cherry tree her mother's window overlooked, eating his lunch, pretending not to be staring right back at her, desperately needing her but knowing to make an attempt to see her would seal both of their fates.

Their fates had been sealed anyway. Cancer had taken care of that first and then the blackness Juan had fallen into had finished the job.

Whatever happened, Catalina was determined not to fall into the same despondency. She had a baby to think about. She'd felt a quickening in her stomach only that morning and a burst of excitement had cut through her, stripping the darkness away for a few, brief magical moments.

She'd felt her baby move. Soon she could expect to feel it kick. Her little miracle of life she would do anything, anything to keep safe. Even if she'd had to give it up.

Because she would have done. And she would be grateful to Nathaniel for ever because now she didn't have to.

He'd lost so much so that she could be a mother to their child and they could both live in freedom. He'd never get his development or the Ravensberg building back but at least the criminal charges against him had been dropped. It still made her furious that, in the aftermath of their escape from the palace, her family had dragged his name through the mud so much so that now his name *was* mud. He didn't deserve that.

'Clotilde?' she called again, then thought she might be having a heart attack when she saw the man rising to his feet from his place on the sofa.

It seemed to take for ever for her brain to comprehend what her eyes were seeing.

'Nathaniel,' she whispered.

She hadn't seen him since the airport. Or spoken to him. They'd communicated in other ways though. Somehow he'd arranged the purchase of this loft for her and opened a bank account in her name, all without actually speaking to her.

He attempted a smile and jammed his hands into his pockets, gazing at her with what seemed like the weight of the world on his shoulders. 'Clotilde has gone out. I hope you don't mind me waiting for you like this?'

'No. No. Of course not. I wasn't expecting you. This is a surprise. How are you?' She didn't know how to stop her tongue from running away with itself.

Now his smile seemed genuine, if sad. 'I'm doing okay.'

'Can I get you a drink?'

'I'm good, thanks. I had a coffee with Clotilde.'

She swallowed and nodded.

'She says you're keeping well.'

'We do our best.' Suddenly she couldn't bear another second of small talk. 'Why are you here?'

'I have something for you.' He pointed to the bureau in the corner. There was a small box on it.

A little dazed, and more than a little confused, hardly able to think straight, she drifted over to it and opened the box. Inside it was jewellery. Catalina's share of her mother's jewellery.

'I didn't want to send it by courier,' he explained, still standing on the same spot in front of the sofa.

She lifted out a rose pendant she had always loved seeing her mother wear and held it to her heart.

Oh, but this meant so much.

Nathaniel had done this for her. He'd rescued her mother's jewellery. Now she'd have something to pass onto their child, something of the beautiful grandmother they would never meet.

'How did you get it?'

'I came to an arrangement with your father.'

'You've been to see him?' she asked, alarmed at the thought.

His lips curved wryly. 'I'm not completely mad. Not yet. No, I sent my lawyer to see him. In exchange for your jewellery I signed an affidavit that I wouldn't take the House of Fernandez to court and sue them for defamation.'

'*Can* you take them to court?' Such a notion had never occurred to her.

He shrugged. 'Your country trades heavily with Europe. There were possibilities. But this was the final straw for your father. Helios has already influenced his Senate into imposing a travel ban on any member of the House of Fernandez entering Agon and was on the verge of imposing a trade embargo on all Monte Cleure goods and finances. The world is opening its eyes to the rottenness behind the throne, so now your father is back in damage limitation mode.'

'Thank you.' It was all she could say. Hot tears had welled in her eyes, which she blinked back. She hadn't cried since the flight to New York. All her tears had dried up.

'I also have a message for you from your father, given via our intermediaries.'

'Oh?'

'He says that if you come home you will be free to live your life as you want.'

'How very kind of him.' She couldn't keep the sarcasm from her voice. 'Does that last until the dust settles and he and Dominic take me back under their control?'

'If that long.'

Their eyes met. They both knew what her father was capable of. They both knew Catalina and their child would never be free if she set foot in her home country again.

'Was there anything else?' she asked, forcing brightness into her voice.

If only she'd been prepared for this visit she would've had time to calm herself down and put her old serene mask back on. She wouldn't be gazing at him, desperately trying to control the urge to throw herself at his feet and beg him to stay.

She wouldn't be howling inside.

'That was everything,' he confirmed quietly. But he made no effort to leave. 'Thank you for the video of the scan.'

She'd asked Clotilde to forward it to him. It hadn't been very clear even though it was taken using the most high-tech 4D scanner available. Their baby had been having far too merry a time playing with its limbs to lie still and pose for them.

'You're welcome.'

Now his feet did move, his legs forming long strides as he headed for the door.

She watched him leave with no words of goodbye. No kiss goodbye. Nothing but the slow ripping of her heart.

She waited to hear the sound of the front door closing so she would be safe to unleash the tears screaming to be released.

Nathaniel stood with his hand on the front door, willing his fingers to work and turn the handle.

He shouldn't have come here. He'd sworn he would drop the jewellery off with Clotilde and leave. But being so close to her...

He couldn't leave without seeing her and witnessing with his own two eyes that she was well.

When he'd sent her to New York he hadn't intended to stay away from her for so long. All he'd cared about was getting her away from Monte Cleure and to safety, then taking some time to process, without her presence there to distract him, what had happened at the party and what he had learned.

Then he'd been told what happened at the airport minutes after he'd left. Catalina had been searching for him, *screaming* for him. She'd been inconsolable.

Her screams had been for him.

The words she'd said before he'd left...*we can be a family...* They'd kept echoing in his ears. Had he misheard her? Misunderstood her?

But he knew he hadn't. Her brave words had been clear.

He hadn't had a family for nearly thirty years.

It came to him then, that if he opened this door and walked out, he would never know...

He would never know if Catalina's screams and distress had been because she...

And now, another bomb dropped on him.

He'd kept his distance because he'd been scared. He'd been scared—terrified—since their first night together. Coming here with her jewellery had been the excuse he'd been searching for without consciously knowing it.

His fears of hurting her...

They were all muddled up. He was scared she would hurt *him*.

If he opened this door...

If he opened this door he would never find out if that family could be...

Suddenly his legs were running back up the stairs and he burst the living-room door open, breathing heavily.

She hadn't moved from the spot by the bureau where he'd left her.

'Were you really preparing to hand our baby to me?' he demanded.

She nodded, her eyes wide, fearful.

'Why?'

'I told you. I couldn't see any other way to keep it safe.'

'And you would have trusted *me* to do that?'

Her eyes were suddenly clear as she answered quietly, 'There's no one else on this earth I would trust more with my baby's life.'

His throat had run dry. 'At the airport, you said I

could come with you and we could be a family. Did you mean that?'

Her bottom lip wobbled and she nodded.

'How do you feel about that now?'

'I…' She swallowed and looked down at the floor.

'Catalina?'

'I still feel the same,' she whispered.

All of a sudden he was standing before her. He didn't remember walking over to her.

Gently, he placed a finger under her chin and raised it so she looked at him.

Chocolate-brown eyes gazed back at him, stark, fearful and *full*.

Now he was the one to swallow. 'I've missed you.'

Her eyes widened.

With his chest threatening to close in on him, he said the words he knew he had to say if he was ever to find the happiness he so badly wanted but had been too scared to take. 'I've been in love with you for ever. It's the only reason I can think of why I decided to develop in your country in the first place. I wanted to be close to you. But I didn't know it.

'I've been running since our first night together but, Lina, I don't think I can run any more. You're in my heart so completely I don't know… I don't know what to do. All I know is that I've never been so scared as when you ran away from me and I've never felt so empty as I have this past month without you. Just standing in the same room as you…it filled some of the emptiness. I told myself I didn't want to hurt you but the truth is you have the power to hurt me and my heart knew it. I've lost everyone I've ever loved before and I was too scared to take that leap of faith. I was scared to admit my love, scared that it would mean I would lose you too.'

He placed his hands on either side of her face and stared deep into her eyes, willing her to *feel* the emotion in his words. 'But if I don't take that leap of faith, how can I ever know? How can *we* ever know? I want to be a family; you, me and our baby, but I haven't had a family for so long... I don't know how to do it.'

He waited for her to say something. Her mouth had opened but no words were coming out.

'If you love me too, please, say it,' he begged her. 'Because I do love you. I need you. I know I don't deserve you or any kind of happiness but...'

'Don't you *ever* say that,' she said, suddenly animated and *fierce*. 'Whatever happened twenty years ago is done with. It's over.' She reached her hands up to cup his cheeks. 'We've both been running away from love. We've only ever known the pain love can bring. You, losing your parents and sister and then your uncle. Me, seeing my mother destroyed by love and experiencing the pain of losing her... Is it any wonder we carry the scars and have been afraid to let love in?

'You're the only man I've ever wanted. You're the only man I've ever loved and the only man I've ever needed. I swore I would never give my heart to anyone, that I would protect it for ever, but you've lodged in there so deep...' She sighed and raised herself onto her toes, and suddenly the mouth he'd been dreaming of for so long was pressed against his and she was breathing him in, and he was breathing her in and in the blink of an eye they were wrapped in each other's arms, pressed so tightly together nothing could prise them apart.

A long, long time later, lying naked together in her bed, limbs entwined, cheeks pressed together, Catalina said softly, 'Neither of us knows how to be a family. You've not had one since before I was born and the example I've had set for me has been about the worst there can be.'

'We'll have to make our version of a family.' He stroked her cheek. 'I didn't think I needed saving but *you've* saved me. You're my world.'

He kissed her again.

It suddenly struck him that he could kiss her for ever.

'I love you,' he said against her mouth.

Her arms hooked around his neck. 'I love you too. Always.'

'Always.'

Always.

EPILOGUE

CLAUDETTE GURGLED.

'Clever girl,' Nathaniel cooed quietly, rubbing his nose against her button one.

His daughter gurgled again and gave a toothless grin.

'Now you must go back to sleep. Mummy needs to rest.'

Another gurgle.

He checked her nappy was dry and sent up a silent prayer of gratitude that she hadn't soiled it while in his charge. He knew Aliana—who had turned up at their New York home out of the blue, announcing she had 'defected' from Monte Cleure—and Clotilde, who had each given themselves the title of nanny, would have happily fought to change it. But night time was private, a time for only him and Catalina and their baby.

He placed Claudette back in her cot, checked the baby monitor, and then tiptoed out of the nursery.

As he climbed back into the warm bed in the room next door, babbling rang out from the monitor, a happy sound he would never tire of listening to.

Catalina turned over and raised a sleepy hand to caress his face. 'Merry Christmas, my love.'

'Merry Christmas, *mon papillon*.'

And for the first time in almost thirty years, Nathaniel knew that this *would* be a merry Christmas. His leap of faith had paid off.

Outside, a snowstorm fell hard, covering the whole of New York in a thick layer of white that would delight all the children waking up to it.

It delighted *him*.

Snow no longer evoked the cruel memories of all he'd lost. His past now only reinforced everything he'd gained. His wife. His daughter. His family.

A fortnight ago, the King had turned up with a full retinue of servants asking if he could meet his granddaughter.

Knowing the King couldn't touch them here—but keeping a healthy amount of security around just in case—they'd let him in and had watched Claudette melt his heart. Well, defrost it a little. When he made noises about them bringing her to Monte Cleure they'd politely refused but had told him he was always welcome to visit Claudette there in New York.

Nathaniel nuzzled into his beautiful wife's neck. 'Do you want your present now?'

'Is it a big present?'

He pressed his growing erection against her thigh. 'Enormous.'

She laughed softly and wrapped her arms around him.

Yes. It was a very merry Christmas indeed.

* * * * *

#3485 THE PRINCE'S PREGNANT MISTRESS

Heirs Before Vows

by Maisey Yates

"I'm pregnant." It takes two words to see Prince Raphael DeSantis bound to a *waitress*. Now to prevent an international incident, Raphael must marry his mistress! But heartsore Bailey won't come willingly. Raphael must seduce Bailey Harper into submission...

#3486 THE GUARDIAN'S VIRGIN WARD

One Night With Consequences

by Caitlin Crews

Domineering Spaniard Izar Agustin couldn't have imagined that his ward, innocent Liliana Girard Brooks, would become such an alluring woman. One night of sensual abandon shows Liliana the unconscious desires of her body... But the consequences of that night bind them together...forever!

#3487 THE DESERT KING'S SECRET HEIR

Secret Heirs of Billionaires

by Annie West

Surrounded by society's glitterati, Arden Wills is confronted with her first and only love, Idris Baddour—a man she never knew was a sheikh! When their ardent kiss is blasted across the world's media, Arden's secret comes to light—the Sheikh has a son!

#3488 SURRENDERING TO THE VENGEFUL ITALIAN

Irresistible Mediterranean Tycoons

by Angela Bissell

Not even his foe's stunning daughter, Helena Shaw, will halt Leonardo Vincenti's vengeance. Leo knows that Helena would never willingly return to his side, so he blackmails her. But the passion that undid them before soon forces them *both* to the brink of surrender...

YOU CAN FIND MORE INFORMATION ON UPCOMING HARLEQUIN® TITLES, FREE EXCERPTS AND MORE AT WWW.HARLEQUIN.COM.

HPCNM1116RB

Natalia Di Sione hasn't left the family estate in years, but she must retrieve her grandfather's lost book of poems from Angelos Menas! The lives of the brooding Greek and his daughter were changed irrevocably by a fire, and Talia finds herself drawn to the formidable tycoon. She knows the untold pleasure Angelos offers is limited, but when she leaves with the book, will her heart remain on the island?

Read on for a sneak preview of
A DI SIONE FOR THE GREEK'S PLEASURE,
the sixth in the unmissable new eight book
Harlequin Presents® series
THE BILLIONAIRE'S LEGACY.

"Talia…" Angelos's voice broke on her name, and then, before she could even process what was happening, he pulled her toward him, his hands hard on her shoulders as his mouth crashed down on hers and plundered its soft depths.

It had been ten years since she'd been kissed, and then only a schoolboy's buss. She'd never been kissed like this, never felt every sense blaze to life, every nerve ending tingle with awareness, nearly painful in its intensity, as Angelos's mouth moved on hers and he pulled her tightly to him.

His hard contours collided against her softness, each point of contact creating an unbearably exquisite ache of longing as she tangled her hands in his hair and fit her mouth against his.

She was a clumsy, inexpert kisser, not sure what to do with her lips or tongue, only knowing that she wanted more of this. Of him.

She felt his hand slide down to cup her breast, his palm hot and hard through the thin material of her dress, and a gasp of surprise and delight escaped her.

That small sound of pleasure was enough to jolt Angelos out of his passion-fogged daze, for he dropped his hand and in one awful, abrupt movement tore his mouth from hers and stepped back.

"I'm sorry," he said, his voice coming out in a ragged gasp.

"No…" Talia pressed one shaky hand to her buzzing lips as she tried to blink the world back into focus. "Don't be sorry," she whispered. "It was wonderful."

"I shouldn't have—"

"Why not?" she challenged. She felt frantic with the desperate need to feel and taste him again, and more important, not to have him withdraw from her, not just physically, but emotionally. Angelos didn't answer and she forced herself to ask the question again. "Why not, Angelos?"

"Because you are my employee, and I was taking advantage of you," he gritted out. "It was not appropriate…"

"I don't care about appropriate," she cried. She knew she sounded desperate and even pathetic but she didn't care. She wanted him. She needed him. "I care about you," she confessed, her voice dropping to a choked whisper, and surprise and something worse flashed across Angelos's face. He shook his head, the movement almost violent and terribly final.

"No, Talia," he told her flatly. "You don't."

Don't miss
A DI SIONE FOR THE GREEK'S PLEASURE,
available December 2016 wherever
Harlequin Presents® books and ebooks are sold.

JUST CAN'T GET ENOUGH
OF THE ALPHA MALE?
Us either!

Come join us at **I Heart Presents** to hear the
latest from your favorite Harlequin Presents
authors and get special behind-the-scenes secrets
of the Presents team!

With access to the latest breaking news and
special promotions, **I Heart Presents** is *the*
destination for all things Presents. Get up close
and personal with the sexy alpha heroes who
make your heart beat faster and share your love
of these glitzy, glamorous reads with the authors,
the editors and fellow Presents fans!

4805

REQUEST YOUR FREE BOOKS!

HARLEQUIN

Presents

2 FREE NOVELS PLUS
2 FREE GIFTS!

PASSION GUARANTEED SEDUCTION

YES! Please send me 2 FREE Harlequin Presents® novels and my 2 FREE gifts (gifts are worth about $10). After receiving them, if I don't wish to receive any more books, I can return the shipping statement marked "cancel." If I don't cancel, I will receive 6 brand-new novels every month and be billed just $4.30 per book in the U.S. or $5.24 per book in Canada. That's a saving of at least 13% off the cover price! It's quite a bargain! Shipping and handling is just 50¢ per book in the U.S. and 75¢ per book in Canada.* I understand that accepting the 2 free books and gifts places me under no obligation to buy anything. I can always return a shipment and cancel at any time. Even if I never buy another book, the two free books and gifts are mine to keep forever.

106/306 HDN GHRP

Name _____ (PLEASE PRINT)

Address _____ Apt. #

City _____ State/Prov. _____ Zip/Postal Code

Signature (if under 18, a parent or guardian must sign)

Mail to the **Reader Service:**
IN U.S.A.: P.O. Box 1867, Buffalo, NY 14240-1867
IN CANADA: P.O. Box 609, Fort Erie, Ontario L2A 5X3

**Are you a current subscriber to Harlequin Presents® books
and want to receive the larger-print edition?
Call 1-800-873-8635 or visit www.ReaderService.com.**

* Terms and prices subject to change without notice. Prices do not include applicable taxes. Sales tax applicable in N.Y. Canadian residents will be charged applicable taxes. Offer not valid in Quebec. This offer is limited to one order per household. Not valid for current subscribers to Harlequin Presents books. All orders subject to credit approval. Credit or debit balances in a customer's account(s) may be offset by any other outstanding balance owed by or to the customer. Please allow 4 to 6 weeks for delivery. Offer available while quantities last.

Your Privacy—The Reader Service is committed to protecting your privacy. Our Privacy Policy is available online at www.ReaderService.com or upon request from the Reader Service.

We make a portion of our mailing list available to reputable third parties that offer products we believe may interest you. If you prefer that we not exchange your name with third parties, or if you wish to clarify or modify your communication preferences, please visit us at www.ReaderService.com/consumerschoice or write to us at Reader Service Preference Service, P.O. Box 9062, Buffalo, NY 14240-9062. Include your complete name and address.

HP15